SAVING THE HOOKER

OTHER TITLES BY MICHAEL ADELBERG

A Thinking Man's Bully

The Razing of Tinton Falls

The American Revolution in Monmouth County

SAVING THE HOOKER

and The Death of the
True-Life Love Story

MICHAEL ADELBERG

THE PERMANENT PRESS
Sag Harbor, NY 11963

Copyright © 2014 by Michael Adelberg

All rights reserved. No part of this publication, or parts thereof, may be reproduced in any form, except for the inclusion of brief quotes in a review, without the written permission of the publisher.

For information, address:
    The Permanent Press
    4170 Noyac Road
    Sag Harbor, NY 11963
    www.thepermanentpress.com

Library of Congress Cataloging-in-Publication Data

Adelberg, Michael—
    Saving the hooker / Michael Adelberg.
        pages cm
    ISBN 978-1-57962-368-5
    1. Academics—Fiction. 2. Prostitutes—Rehabilitation—New York (State)—New York—Fiction. 3. Escort services—New York (State)—New York—Fiction. 4. Man-woman relationships—Fiction. I. Title.

PS3601.D4666S37 2014
813'.6—dc23   2013043539

Printed in the United States of America

This book is dedicated to the compassionate people at Magdalene in Nashville, HIPS in Washington, DC, Destiny House in Las Vegas, and similar programs in other places, who are helping at-risk young people choose something other than sexual trafficking.

CONTENTS

Dear Reader   9

CHAPTER 1   Saving the Hooker   13

CHAPTER 2   Two Smart Fellows, They Felt Smart   20

CHAPTER 3   The Happy Hooker   32

CHAPTER 4   Wee Willy and Tiny Tim   47

CHAPTER 5   Betting on the Cum   61

CHAPTER 6   Linner with My Frenemy   72

CHAPTER 7   Through Hook or Crook   85

CHAPTER 8   Depraving the Hooker   92

CHAPTER 9   The Odds are Good, but the Goods are Odd   102

CHAPTER 10   Where the Third World Meets the Nerd World   117

CHAPTER 11   Champagne for My Real Friend and Real Pain for My Sham Friend   128

CHAPTER 12   Purple Jesus and Black Santa   140

CHAPTER 13   Membership has Its Privileges   153

CHAPTER 14   Adequate is the New Excellent   171

CHAPTER 15   It's Cheaper to Keep Her   180

CHAPTER 16   The War with the Whore   192

Life after Death   200

Dear Reader

My name is Matthew Hristahalios (pronounced: Hrist-a-hal-E-Os) and I'm writing this letter fifteen minutes after my fifteen minutes of fame chaotically ended.

I'm now on a six-month writing sabbatical. The sabbatical is unpaid, but room and board are provided free of charge. My sabbatical is being hosted by the Otisville Correctional Facility in New York. *Forbes* magazine recently named Otisville one of the ten best places in the United States to go to prison and I believe it. The sheets are clean, there's basic cable in the common areas, and the food's on par with Denny's. I have only two gripes with being here: First, the computer in my room—nobody at Otisville says "cell"—is equipped with only Microsoft Word 97 and cannot read my research files. So I've had to retype a ton of work from scratch. Second, the prison has a clique of Orthodox Jewish occupants—nobody at Otisville says "inmates"—whose temple is just down the hall from me. Much as I try to ignore it, I find the hard "ch" sound of the Hebrew language distracting; it is impossible to focus on my writing during their daily services.

But back to my fifteen minutes of fame: I'm that guy whom Keith Olbermann called "The Worst Person in the World." Bill O'Reilly called me a "Pinhead of the Highest Order" during his *Pinheads and Patriots* segment. David Letterman devoted a top-ten list to me: "Top Ten Lies from that Sad-Sack Hooker Guy." Even talk-news personality Eliot

Spitzer, the former governor brought down by a hooker scandal, took a shot at me:

> Mr. Hristahalios, this is serious. Think about yourself—a young professor—in prison with real criminals. But knowing something of your money troubles, maybe that's not all bad. At least the sex will be free this time around.

Yes, fourteen minutes of my fifteen minutes of fame were spent as the butt of jokes. I can live with that. But I can't live with the three people who should know better than thinking they have the right to be angry with me.

Randall Skiles, PhD, parlayed his minor role in my televised flameout into a 500-word letter to the editor in the *New York Times* and an appearance on public television. He feigned sympathy for me, noting "the horrible pressures Matthew faced within the crucible of academia," but all he really did was self-promote his WASP looks and patrician diction. Now he's hosting a talk show on public radio devoted to giving voice to postdocs and other young scholars. It's called something incredibly lame like *Scholarly Styles with Randy Skiles*. What a dick.

And then there's Julia Roberts. No, not the actress—I'm talking about the downtown Manhattan prostitute who uses the same name. Her profanity-laden tirade against me on national television launched her fifteen minutes of fame. This summer, you'll be able to see her five nights a week at midnight on *E!* They gave her a reality show, *The Madness of Julia Roberts*. Before she met me, she was nothing but a hooker with a coke problem. She sent me to the emergency room and robbed me, and, like a sucker, I never went to the police about it. Then, when I lost my temper with her, she grabbed a lawyer and threw the kitchen sink at me. She should be kissing my ass; of course, if she did, she'd insist that I owe her another $200.

Even my father, Al Hristahalios, a modest man who never would have asked for fifteen minutes of fame, prospered from my humiliation. In exchange for discussing my prolonged virginity on Howard Stern's radio show, Stern plugged his business to a national audience. Dad rebuilds truck engines and installs them into restored and classic big rigs. His orders have doubled since Stern called out www.RESTOREMYDIESEL.com to millions of listeners. Now that I've also plugged Dad's business, maybe he'll knock off the wounded parent routine and answer one of my e-mails.

I sit in jail for a hodgepodge of pseudocrimes committed against three people who've gained from my misfortune. Still, I'm the monster.

It's time to set the record straight. I hope you'll enjoy *Saving the Hooker.*

CHAPTER 1

Saving the Hooker

I was seven when Dad brought home a videocassette of the movie *Pretty Woman* for Mom. She insisted that we watch it as a family. The three of us settled onto the couch. I don't remember much about the movie, but I do remember my parents arguing after Richard Gere vanquished scheming Jason Alexander and swept up Julia Roberts.

As the credits rolled and Roy Orbison sang, Mom leaned over me and kissed Dad on the cheek. She told him she loved the movie.

Dad, who had served 20 years in the army in southern Italy and Vietnam, said, "Hon, glad you liked it, but this is one of the dumbest movies ever made. I spent time with some hookers while in the service." He chuckled, "They aren't even a little bit like Julia Roberts. This movie's just a Prince Charming fairy tale for little girls."

And then things got hot. They said terrible things about each other, using code words that I now understand were references to each other's unfulfilled ambitions and sexual fantasies. I squished down in the couch cushions between them—hoping they would stop.

Finally, Mom ended the discussion. She picked up the VCR remote control and froze the screen on the closing movie credits: "Well, Al, read the credits. Director – Garry Marshall; Producers – Arnon Milchan, Gary W. Goldstein, and Steven Reuther; Writer – Jon Frederick Lawton; Cinematographer – Charles Minsky: All are men. This movie might be a fairy tale, but it's a fairy tale by horny men—high-paid losers. I bet they all beat off to Julia Roberts during the casting. It's why she got the role. They still think about her in that short skirt when they have to get it up for their wives. I can't believe you don't love this movie, Al. Maybe I'll get lucky tonight. It's been two weeks."

Mom won that argument. She won every argument with Dad. She was always the sharp-tongued parent—the one willing to escalate a disagreement to a meaner level. But her comments about *Pretty Woman* were more than a trump card in a domestic squabble. Mom offered brilliant film criticism.

If Mom hadn't grown up in a trailer park, married a man she never loved, and had a kid at 19, she might have been an amazing critic. Mom could have been so many things had she not been assigned to live in Morris, Illinois, the dullest place on Earth—had she not died before her son could help her.

Mom's line about *Pretty Woman* lodged in some dusty corner of my brain, and reappeared three years ago when I was watching *The Hangover*, the defining guys' movie of this century. There she was again—the Julia Roberts character from *Pretty Woman* reincarnated as Heather Graham's character in *The Hangover*: Hot, fun, street smart, and a really sweet person. The only thing keeping Heather Graham from being perfect was that she needed that nice dentist, Ed Helms, to rescue her from hooking. A man had to make an "honest" woman of her. Graham's hooker, like Julia Roberts's hooker a generation earlier, was the most virtuous and competent character in the movie. But still only a man could save her.

This started me on a little quest to examine hookers in other American stories. I spent the spring of 2012 doing only two things: 1. writing my postdoc application to the Manhattan University Center for Interdisciplinary Studies, and 2. watching movies with hooker characters. From my little apartment in Brooklyn Heights, I waited every day for the mailman to bring me more Netflix DVDs with more hookers to examine. I invented a second identity and opened a second Netflix account just so I could order more movies with prostitutes.

When not watching hooker movies, I read about them. I read maybe ten books about prostitutes and found dozens of American stories built around the heroic man "saving" the fallen woman—not just dime-store novels, but classics like Stephen Crane's *Maggie: A Girl of the Streets* and George Bernard Shaw's *Pygmalion*.

Even the producers of the HBO pseudodocumentary *Cat House* bought into the myth, including (*faux?*) confessions from prostitutes speaking wistfully about the special man who might one day bring them out of hooking. Across the decades, the plot kept recycling: The attractive street woman saved by a good man.

I made myself an expert on the "hooker with a heart of gold" in the American Western. Five times I watched *Stagecoach*, and five times I watched John Wayne ride off into the sunset at the end of the movie with Marlene Dietrich, the saved hooker. I watched a dozen Westerns costarring Marie Windsor and Ann Dvorak, buxom women always cast as prostitutes or dance hall girls. The character they played was always the same: The sexy, smart talkin', streetwise woman awaiting redemption through a heroic man.

I found the same hooker in modern cinema: Jamie Lee Curtis's Ophelia in *Trading Places*, Rebecca De Mornay's Lana in *Risky Business*. And then I watched *Pretty Woman* again and understood why, despite its chick-flick reputation, so many men secretly love it. I masturbated to Julia Roberts that night—and dozens of nights since.

It was June 28, 2012. My application to the center was due on June 30. It was half-completed and not very good. I was writing about how suburbanization, with its long commuting lifestyle, changed the American book. But I had no provable thesis or research approach. I was past desperate; self-loathing was setting in for having wasted the entire spring on my hooker obsession.

With no other choice, I scrapped my half-baked post-doc proposal and rewrote a new one from scratch:

Saving the Hooker:

Juxtaposing the Hooker with a Heart of Gold in American Media

with the Actual Women of the Sex Trade

The research would be divided into two parts: First, I would conduct an extensive literature review to document the archetypical hooker depicted in American books and visual media (this was already largely done, but they didn't need to know that). Second, I would interview a cross section of real hookers, examine their pathologies, and determine the degree to which they can be "saved" by a caring man and the frayed social safety net of modern America. I would examine the dissonance between the mythic hooker of *Pretty Woman, et al*, and the real thing.

In ten powerfully argued pages, I proposed to discuss the virtuous hooker archetype in American storytelling, and contrast it against prostitution as a deep-seated societal problem. I proposed to introduce these women to healthier behaviors and provide caring, platonic companionship. I would be Richard Gere to Julia Roberts, John Wayne to Marlene Dietrich, but without heroes, villains, or movie climaxes. I would work from protocols ground in established qualitative research methodologies and make the best possible use of existing social services to help these women. My efforts would be rigorously documented for scholarly purposes.

Competition was fierce for postdocs at the center. Thirty applicants were vying for two slots, but my *Saving the Hooker* proposal was the best paper I'd ever written.

August 7, 2012, was the happiest day of my life. I was selected for the postdoc. It meant so many things all at once: Recognition as a promising scholar, two more years with a life-sustaining stipend, and two more years to pursue my hooker obsession—now legitimized by real scholarship. I celebrated by indulging myself with a little companionship. I bought a cute little parrot whom I named Harpo. I vowed to teach him a funny line or two that would crack up visitors from home—because every hayseed from rural Illinois wants to visit the Big Apple.

I e-mailed the news of the fellowship to the half-dozen professors who'd been helpful to me during my six years of grad work at New York University. I also e-mailed the good news to a few friendly grad school colleagues who'd moved on to faculty positions at small colleges in the middle of the country.

Then I stopped. There was no one else I wanted to tell; my social circle was pitifully small and shrinking. Sure, I still had my two old high school buddies from Illinois—Will and Tim—but they'd have no idea what I was talking about. They'd kid me about studying hookers to get free blow jobs.

I was out of people I wanted to tell, but there still was someone I had to tell. There was still Dad: Dad who gets his information from right-wing talk-news programs and spends his evenings promoting hair-brained petitions on the Internet. Without any joy, I forwarded him the e-mail announcement. Then I dialed the phone.

Conversation with Dad: August 9, 2012

"What dumb-ass is paying you to study that?" Dad asked with typical sensitivity. Nobody plays the part of the blunt-speaking everyman as well as Dad.

"A committee of past fellows from the Center for Interdisciplinary Studies annually peer select two projects that they believe will advance scholarship in the construction of identities in American culture. They select two new fellows each year. I know this isn't your thing, Dad. I'm not studying the NFL's most bone-jarring hits or the raunchiest lines from *Family Guy*. But still it's important and interesting."

"Hey look, Matty, I know you're a bright guy. I'm just trying to understand what you'll be doing. You're 28 and still never worked a real job. According to this e-mail from your center, you're now going to spend two years watching movies and reading books to learn about hookers. I haven't been near a hooker in thirty years, but I know that you don't read books to find out about them."

"That's not quite right, Dad. I'm going to look at the hooker as a cultural archetype. Think about the prostitutes of the 1940s Westerns, then think about Julia Roberts in *Pretty Woman* and Heather Graham in *The Hangover*. American men continue to portray hookers as something quite unreal. The hooker is sexy, wise, and invariably virtuous. I will interview actual prostitutes and provide them opportunities to improve their lives—or at least to bridge into safer and healthier lifestyles. I will show the incoherence between the mythic hooker of the male storyteller and the real women who ply the sex trade."

There was a pause. "Jeez, Matty, you can even make hookers boring."

Dad's good for a few put-downs before his conscience kicks in and reminds him that a good parent must be supportive of his child. So I was not surprised by his next line: "Well your, uh, project sounds interesting. So these people at this center will pay your freight for two more years to do this studying of story-time and real hookers. Then you'll write about it."

"Yes, Dad, two years. It's a postdoc—an extended period of time pursuing a single research topic beyond my dissertation. The center received thirty applications and made only two selections. It's a real affirmation of my work. It says that I'm a promising scholar. It lines me up for publishing my research into a book, tenure-track faculty positions, and National Endowment for the Humanities grants."

"Well, if you were building something like your old man, I could see the worth of what you're doing a lot better. But, Matty, you know that I'm proud of you. I'm sure your mother's smiling too—even if you believe she's just a piece of meat in the ground being eaten by worms." He paused, his voice tight for a moment.

He continued, "Before your mother died, it was her job to worry about you. Now I worry. Getting involved with New York City hookers is going to take you to places you don't yet understand—ugly places. Maybe you'll write the best book ever about hookers, but it will come at a price. These hookers won't be like the girls you grew up with. Matty, you don't know what you're getting yourself into."

"Thanks for your concerns, Dad, but I'll be fine. It's just research. I'll call you in a couple of weeks."

The conversation went better than I had expected.

CHAPTER 2

Two Smart Fellows, They Felt Smart

So now I was a fellow. In the three weeks between being notified of my selection and the welcome reception, I didn't do very much. Mostly, I kept watching movies about hookers, beating off to the sexy ones, and sleeping through New York's miserable August weather. I justified the indolence by telling myself that I'd soon be working incredibly hard and needed to bank some sleep and down time.

My first official responsibility as a fellow was attending the annual reception with the center's faculty and past fellows. At this reception, my selection and the selection of the other 2013 fellow would be officially announced.

The morning of the reception, I rolled out of bed and performed my morning rituals: Two sets of push-ups to keep my arms toned and ten minutes with Harpo repeating the statement "birds can't talk" for his eventual memorization. I showered and looked in the mirror. There was some good news: Despite six years of geekdom, I was still okay-looking. I had a full head of wavy dark hair on a broad-shouldered six-foot frame. The acne that dogged me into my twenties was finally gone. My upper body still showed the effects of three years of high school football and wrestling. I still could do four chin-ups in a row on a good day. But the good news ended there.

I opened my closet and confirmed what I already knew. I had nothing appropriate to wear. The uniform for an academic dinner is well known: Tweed jacket or navy blazer over a white button shirt and well-pressed khaki pants. I had plenty of pants, none well pressed, and most too tight to button. Reluctantly, I unzipped the suit bag at the far right corner of the closet and pulled it out. It contained the black pinstriped business suit Dad bought for me two years ago when I mistakenly told him I was thinking about leaving academia to get a real job.

The suit pants were tight in the butt, and the jacket didn't button easily, but it was good enough. At least I had black dress socks and matching black business shoes. Sure I looked more Wall Street than Ivy League, but it was a coherent ensemble. Some old-school faculty might even appreciate that I was overdressed. There really was no alternative. After a shower and a shave, I was out the door and on the subway into Manhattan.

The New York City subways have come a long way from the grime and graffiti of the 1980s, but the cars still are abused by a ridership that is disinterested in their upkeep. I boarded a car that was randomly dotted with some kind of paint. A large mass of spilled Slurpee inched backward as the train rolled, and then crashed forward into the car's front wall at each stop. The light blue frozen goop slathered halfway up the car's front wall. The car was near empty. It was four on Thursday afternoon and I was riding against traffic. The other five riders were black—two young mothers with three ill-governed children.

The train jostled and lurched through a half-dozen downtown Manhattan stops, including Union Square, my long-time stop for NYU. After this stop, the train took on passengers. It was close and steamy by the time it trudged into midtown. I was hemmed in on both sides by jostling sweaty riders. Finally, I reached my stop at Forty-Second Street.

Times Square in August at five thirty is a collision of smells. People from all over the world are released from service jobs. They carry into the street the lingering effects of curry lunches and deodorant-deprived armpits. These smells mix with the city street's own two pervasive odors, car exhaust and urine. Thirty feet above ground level, Times Square is Disneyfied and perfectly packaged for whitebread America—the great triumph of Rudy Giuliani's urban renewal. But at street level, at the start of rush hour, Times Square still combines the worst elements of Sodom and the Tower of Babel.

I passed the Port Authority Bus Terminal and the tens of thousands it releases to New Jersey each evening. After that, the masses thinned and the last two blocks to the center were quite pleasant. This neighborhood, the mid-Forties on the west side, was once called Hell's Kitchen. It was known for its gangs of tough Polish and Puerto Rican kids—the neighborhood inspired *West Side Story*. Now, like all of Manhattan's once troubled residential areas, it's traded up. At five forty-five P.M., the sidewalks are dotted with young professional women, harried but still attractive in their charcoal skirts, rushing home to relieve their Latina nannies by six. Their husbands, though earning less money, disappear with buddies for a couple of beers before coming home. The businesswomen steal glances at their iPhones as they briskly walk past me and bound up the stairs of their brownstones.

The center sits on Eleventh Avenue near the Hudson River, far removed from the graduate school's main campus in the middle of midtown's swirl of traffic and noise. I remember Dr. Anthony Beckwith, the center's director, telling me about how the graduate school came to acquire the property. A neighborhood boy from Hell's Kitchen made a ton of money in the '60s on real estate in New Jersey. Feeling nostalgic, he bought his old childhood brownstone and two adjacent brownstones. Then he knocked out the adjoining walls. But he never finished his grand plan for the property. When he died, his kids—safely swaddled in suburbia—didn't want to deal with the eccentric property.

So they gifted it to Manhattan University for a handsome charitable tax deduction, and the university gave it to the graduate school. Beckwith and a half-dozen history and sociology professors on the outs with their departments accepted exile away from the main campus. They were pleased to have their own place to pursue American studies, a scholarly *cul-de-sac* devoted to such critical topics as television news, fast food, and video games—those things that create our singular American popular culture.

The center's receptionist—a handsome Indian woman named Jayaprada—buzzed me in. I made some small talk with her, and made her laugh by slipping into the New England brogue of Dr. Beckwith. I put my butt on her desk, "Hey, why don't you stay for tonight's reception. You can be my guest." She looked down, "Thank you, but I need to go home to my parents right after work. They are not well." My first attempt at asking out a girl in two years produced the predictable result.

The reception and dinner were being hosted in the center's so-called "concourse," a fifty-foot room spanning the three brownstones, but breached by two rows of load-bearing columns. Usually, the concourse hosts graduate seminars with long tables arranged around the columns in a U-shape. In that capacity, it is never more than half-full. But this night the concourse held ten round tables with eight chairs each. The air conditioning struggled to cool the packed room. There was a flimsy podium at the front with a microphone stand.

Dr. Beckwith came across the room and extended his hand. "Matthew, I was just bowled over by your proposal. I was reading it over the summer and said to myself, 'This is the one—the perfect balance of humanities and social science. He's onto something.' When you were in my seminar, I wondered about your commitment to American studies—but now, well, I welcome you to the Center for Interdisciplinary Studies. I am looking forward to proctoring your research over the next two years." He gave me an envelope. "Your first semester stipend is in here, as well as $1,500 in cash for the incidental costs of conducting your interviews. You'll get future checks from Jayaprada on the committee's approval of your budgets. Congratulations."

For three years, I'd known Dr. Anthony Beckwith as an indifferent lecturer, aloof researcher, and meticulous editor of *The American Journal of American Studies*. In this brief reintroduction, he'd spoken more words to me than during the entire semester in which I was enrolled in his graduate seminar, *Suburban Sods: the Grand Conceit of the American Lawn*.

"Thank you, Dr. Beckwith, it is an honor to be selected for the fellowship. I won't let you or the committee down." Beckwith led me over to a modest wine and cheese spread where I was introduced to three previous fellows. I politely listened to them gossip about the fellow from two years ago who was tossed out of the program for underperforming.

The conversation shifted to the projects of the previous fellows: A gangly woman, named Meriboe, used the fellowship to write "The Redneck Panorama, from Montana to Alabama: An Annotated Taxonomy of Contemporary, Rural White Subcultures between the Rocky and the Appalachian Mountains"; a Canadian named Colin wrote "Lionizing the Lion: The Correlating Rise of Predatory Mammal Iconography with Declining Anglo-American Global Power"; and a 2007 fellow, a petite woman named Naomi, wrote "From Sacajawea to Saccharine: An Interdisciplinary Examination of America's Obsession with Sweetness." Each fellow's paper was now a scholarly monograph published by a second- or third-tier academic press. Their three books were lined up on a table behind the podium with a dozen others from past fellows. As I made small talk with the three past fellows, I lied about reading chapters of their books, and promised to read each in its entirety.

They nodded politely and promised to read my work when it published. We all understood this would never happen.

One former fellow—a distinctly feminine-looking woman desperately trying to look androgynous in her short hair and quasi-military blazer—kept her distance from me as I mixed with the other fellows. Twice, we made eye contact. Both times I received a sour look. As I separated from the other fellows to get a drink, I came up to her.

"Hello," I nodded.

She nodded, but stayed silent.

"I'm Matthew Hristahalios, one of this year's fellows." I extended my hand.

"I know," she said, but she did not extend hers.

"Have I done anything to offend you?"

"As a matter of fact, yes, you have."

"Well, please tell me what I've done. I don't even know you."

"I'm Jess Wurge, a fellow from 2006. I was on the selection panel for this year's fellowships. I was dead against your project—it is fundamentally misogynistic. But I was outvoted."

"I don't think I understand. My proposal freely acknowledges the sexism inherent in the 'hooker with a heart of gold' archetype. It's based on the sexism at the core of the archetype."

"Oh sure, but that's like saying the sky is blue." She pivoted to face me. "Tell me this: Why do you think you can save women? Maybe women don't want to be saved. Or maybe they don't want to be saved by whatever male bourgeois measures you've applied to that term. Or maybe these women do want to be saved, but not by a man like you. Or maybe it's kind of a stupid idea to test whether a man can save a woman. Maybe only certain kinds of men can save certain kinds of women. Maybe women should be saving men? Most of the men I know need some saving. You were lucky to draw a panel with four men and only one woman—me. It's no surprise that the men all loved your proposal."

I wanted to fire back. I knew that some liberal arts-campus feminist somewhere eventually would come after me. I had a well-rehearsed counterattack: "Well, Helen Reddy, maybe you should just take it easy. This is an American studies postdoc, not the Women's Suffrage movement. The stakes are kind of low here. Sorry my research offends you. I guess it was going to offend someone—that's how things work within the modern Outrage Industrial Complex."

But I lost my nerve, and simply mumbled: "You could be a little nicer to strangers."

She took her drink and walked off.

Beckwith returned with his arm around a tall, fit, blue-blood looking guy. His blond hair swooped down, covering the center of his forehead. He wore wire rim glasses, a camel-colored jacket, perfectly pressed dark brown pants, and an open-collar white linen shirt. It was the perfect academic uniform.

"Matthew Hristahalios," Beckwith said, "I would like you to meet Randall Skiles, this year's other fellow selection. You and Randall will be neighbors and colleagues for the next two years."

Randall Skiles extended a big hand toward me. "Hrist-O-hal-E-Os" Skiles said slowly. "That's a bit of a tongue twister, but my Peace Corps years among the Yoruba taught my tongue to handle any combination of sounds—whether Equatorial African or Aegean." He winked at Beckwith.

Now I winked at Beckwith. "Well, my name is a bit of a tongue twister, like 'One smart fellow'. Although, Randall, I guess we're two smart fellows. You know, as in the tongue twister:

> "One smart fellow, he felt smart;
> "two smart fellows, they felt smart;
> "three smart fellows, they all *smelled fart*."

I laughed as my tongue fell errantly over itself on the last line. Beckwith and Skiles stared at me.

Skiles cleared his throat. "Oh, yes, I see. Flatulence humor, very charming. Well, Hristahalios, I will always be pleased to assist you in any way I can." Beckwith nodded approvingly. I already hated Randall Skiles.

An hour later, the reception dinner began. Dr. Skiles and I were officially introduced to the audience of past fellows and faculty. Although I had not written down any comments, I took my place behind the podium comfortably to offer some remarks about my project: "My friends, research from the National Task Force on Prostitution suggests that 1.5 million American women have sold sexual favors at some point in the lives; 60 percent of those women have been victims of physical violence. A study of prostitution from the University of Chicago tells us that most prostitutes have substance-abuse problems, and the rate of mental illness in this population is ten times that of the general female population. And yet the male-dominated media perpetuates a view of a very different prostitute: We are treated to Julia Roberts of *Pretty Woman* and Heather Graham of *The Hangover*—women who are sexy, fun, savvy, kindhearted, and compassionate. We see prostitutes who are empowered and self-actualized in every way except one—they are locked into prostitution. And they can only be saved by a man. Prince Charming is the only person capable of saving the 'hooker with a heart of gold.' Friends, I will spend the next two years documenting the dissonance between the real and the imagined prostitute, and determine the degree to which real prostitutes are willing to be, or capable of being, saved."

I received an appropriate round of applause. Beckwith nodded approvingly. I sat down.

Randy Skiles was introduced next. He patted my back as he passed me on the way to the podium and unfolded a small piece of paper. "Good evening, friends, fellows and distinguished faculty. I'm not going to try to impress you with statistics from a national commission [muffled laughter from the audience]. I just want to briefly tell you about two young females who were both the victims of terrible kidnappings in the last decade. In June 2003, a cute-as-a-button fourteen-year-old blonde was held at knifepoint, taken from her Utah home, and kidnapped. The girl, Elizabeth Smart, was found nine months later after a national media firestorm. I imagine many of you remember her? [Nodding heads in the audience.] In March 2011, an attractive nineteen-year-old college student was kidnapped at gunpoint by four men from her cousin's New Jersey home. A month later, her body turned up in the Schuylkill River in Philadelphia. The girl's name was Nadirah Ruffin . . . and no one in this room has ever heard of her. She was black. Elizabeth Smart was white. Jon Benet Ramsey was white. Chandra Levy was white. Patty Hearst was white. The Lindbergh baby was white. Every kidnapping victim you can name was white. Visit the Wikipedia page for famous kidnappings and you'll find thirty victims listed—all are white."

A hush fell over the room. Randy had everyone's attention, even mine.

"Colleagues, today we live in a society that is increasingly characterized as postracial. Interracial marriages are way up; we have a black president—all good things. Yet, our media still sells us *Leave it to Beaver* every night on the news, using sensational crime stories with white victims as the touchstone. I will spend the next two years documenting the persistent news media bias against minorities and interviewing people across the media in an attempt to determine the degree to which this bias is unintentional and subliminal and the degree to which it is an intentional ratings-driven strategy based on the belief that a white majority identifies with white children more than children of color."

Randy Skiles returned to his seat. When he sat down, he was the only one in the room sitting. Everyone else was giving him a standing ovation.

I drank nine or ten glasses of wine before taking the train home that evening.

Conversation with Dad: August 26, 2012

The phone rang, and rang and rang. Finally, I picked it up.

"Whoever you are, why are you calling so early?" I coughed into the phone.

"Well someone had it rough last night. I've already been out for my morning jog and dropped a rebuild into a '77 Mack. And remember, it's an hour earlier here in Illinois. Christ, it's eleven in New York. Rise and shine, Sonny Boy."

The only thing worse than Dad in a bad mood is Dad in a good mood.

"Okay, Dad, so it's not really early. Sorry. But I'm kind of wiped out. Can I call you back?"

"Uh, sure Matt. Sorry your father is such a bother. Hey, did you see my latest petition to Obama on petition.com? You have to sign it."

"Jeez, Dad. Why do you do that stuff? Stop watching Wolf News. What right-wing cause are they getting you riled up about now?"

"You got me wrong. My favorite Wolf News show is *The Daily Howl* and most of their stuff isn't even political. It's just common sense reporting, and the host, Marie, is sure a firecracker . . . Anyway, this week's petition isn't political. It's just fun—and it's short. I can read it to you:

> President Obama: Please nuke the moon. We have to nuke something, so why not our own moon? It'll keep the Russkies and Richard Branson from going there.

I tried not to laugh, but couldn't hold back the snort and snicker. "Yes that's funny, Dad. I will sign that petition."

"Hey, I remember from that e-mail you sent that you had your coronation yesterday, that big shindig about your fellowship. I wanted to know if you got to meet the Queen of England, or at least your new professors. I want to hear what these people think about your writing about hookers. Tell me about your new classes."

"Jesus, Dad, this is a postdoc. I have my PhD. I'll be researching prostitutes for two years under the supervision of a committee of former fellows and professors. I'm done with classes."

"What about friends, Matt? Will you be with anyone your own age?"

"There's one other fellow. He's about my age . . . maybe a couple of years older."

"Good, you could use a little companionship. New York may be the world's biggest city, but it still can be a very lonely place."

"It's not the world's biggest city, Dad. That's Mexico City. Tokyo and Shanghai are bigger than New York, too."

"Bullshit. No way Mexico City's bigger than New York. Half of Mexico lives here in the United States. Anyway, I'm just glad you'll have a friend to share a beer with after school."

"Sure, Dad. I look forward to watching *Dukes of Hazzard* reruns while tipping back some Miller High Lifes with him. He's a real 'Miller Time' kind of guy." I groaned a little. "My head hurts. I'll call you next week."

CHAPTER 3

The Happy Hooker

For the next week, I moped around the center by day and my apartment by night. I was still finding new material to read about hookers, but hadn't started any real research. Five times, I exited the subway at Canal Street and walked toward the Holland Tunnel entrance. I watched the prostitutes come out at sunset. I recognized two regulars—one black and probably transsexual, the other a beautiful young Latina. For four nights, I imagined introducing myself to Ms. Caliente and telling her that I was a researcher. I imagined buying her a cup of coffee and talking with her about Mexico and how she fell into hooking. I imagined her telling me that I was the first truly nice man she'd ever known. But I didn't come within fifty feet of her. My lifelong shyness around women and Dad's warning about New York City hookers made me afraid of them. With my luck, Ms. Caliente would just walk away, while the black tranny would feel me up with her man hands.

Finally, on the fifth night, I came in contact with the prostitutes. As the tranny bent herself into a car window, Ms. Caliente called over to me. "Hey Meester. You like what you see? I see you watching me all the time."

"Huh. Who me? No, I mean yes. Watching. I mean you no harm." I was spasming nonsense words.

"Harm?" She looked at me like I was from Mars. She crossed the street toward me. I now could see acne on her face—she looked younger as she came close. Was she even eighteen?

I screwed up my courage. "Can I buy you a cup of coffee?"

"No coffee, man, but we can party? You like to party? I like to party with guys like you." She was only twenty feet away.

I went silent.

She stopped. "Something wrong with you, man? I like to party, you know. You like to party. We party together."

I couldn't bring myself to say anything.

"Come on, Beebee," the tranny called out. "He's a looker, not a buyer. Cheap-ass perv. Leave him alone. I got a couple of buyers here."

Ms. Caliente promptly turned and recrossed Canal Street. She and the tranny piled into a car with heavily tinted windows and sped off.

At the end of week one of the fellowship, I composed my first weekly progress report for the committee. It wasn't much—a page and a half summary of my readings and prepreliminary thoughts on the interview protocol I would use for interviewing prostitutes. That weekend, I received an e-mail from Dr. Beckwith telling me to meet with him on Monday. His summons couldn't be good news. It was only a question of how bad the news might be.

On Monday, I put off getting on the subway until three, narrowing the window of opportunity for arriving at the center before Beckwith's usual departure at four thirty. It was an unusually warm day for September and I jogged the last four blocks to reach the center by four fifteen. My face was red and armpits sweaty when I reached the center. Jayaprada looked away as I entered—I was now a leper for showing some interest in her. The building was warm and muggy because the air conditioning had been shut off for the year as part of the university's austerity program. It was even worse on the third floor of the brownstone where Beckwith had a cramped office made more cramped by waist-high piles of books and journals that grew up like stalagmites from the floor.

He was staring out into the hallway at me as I came up. My clunking shoes on the rickety wood stairs made it impossible to sneak up on him. It made knocking on his door superfluous.

Beckwith, a large man with a natural slouch that made him look like a turtle, tipped his face forward, his double chin resting on his chest. He spoke from his chair. "Come in, Matthew."

"Thank you, Dr. Beckwith, when I saw your e-mail, I wanted to come right away. But I needed to finish some reading today."

"Oh, I am sure it was something very timely," Beckwith offered in a voice that barely feigned sincerity. "Tell me about your first report to the committee, the one you submitted on Friday. How might you want me, as your committee chair, to receive it?"

By the deferential standards of academia, this was a pretty direct question. I am sure Beckwith intended to convey dissatisfaction.

"Well, ah-ah-ah, I'm simply starting my project by grounding myself fully in the pertinent literature." I then offered a string of facts detailing different movie prostitutes. Beckwith looked disinterested as I prattled on about the "hooker with a heart of gold."

"Matthew, I'm not saying it is the case here, but mastering all the literature can become an excuse for not beginning your research. Over the years, a few fellows have fallen into this trap—one of whom had to be terminated despite his outstanding potential. So now I am more vigilant. Tell me when you'll be ready to begin your qualitative field research with prostitutes. I can have the IRB review your interview protocol and research plan in short order. Since you are a postdoc, I can bump you ahead in the queue. The unwritten rules of the Internal Review Board favor fellows with time-limited funding—we all recognize the need to get you into the field quickly. If your submissions are in order, I can get you through IRB within two weeks."

"That's super news Dr. Beckwith because I spent the weekend drafting my interview questions, and think the full protocol is rounding into shape quite nicely," I lied. I promised him a package for IRB by week's end and rose to get out of his office as fast as possible.

"Matthew, one more thing, I think you'd be well served by informally meeting some of the women you'll be studying. It will help you focus your protocol and perhaps get you past any initial, ah, uneasiness you might be feeling right now. I want you to contact Rachel Rubenstein. She teaches in the School of Social Work over at the Forty-Second Street campus. Rachel has, among other things, won grants to provide services to prostitutes and other at-risk women and she's brought in prostitutes to speak to her students. I think she could be helpful to you. Shortly before you arrived this afternoon, I e-mailed Rachel and copied you on my note. I told her to expect a visit from you this week."

Beckwith's head came up from his chest. "I trust you'll be prompt in contacting Dr. Rubenstein."

I heard myself say, "Yes, tomorrow."

By the time I made it back to my apartment that evening, Professor Rubenstein already had responded to Beckwith's e-mail, saying that she'd be happy to speak with me and listing her office hours. Beckwith had replied, "Thank you Rachel. I'm sure Matthew will see you tomorrow."

THE MAIN grad school campus on Forty-Second is the quintessential high-rise academic building—classrooms dominate the lower twenty floors, faculty offices the upper twenty. Paper flyers for token causes—save the tiger, save Tibet, save paper, save the Tibetan Paper Tiger—litter the hallways. I entered the elevator and pressed thirty-eight. Exiting the elevators and turning left, I passed no less than fifteen office doors, all closed, before reaching Rubenstein's open door. I waited in the hall, listening to a weepy undergrad protest a grade. When the disgruntled student stormed out, I entered.

Rubenstein looked the part of the aging hippie—long graying ponytail, oversized peasant blouse, and loose cotton pants. As I sat down, I wondered what she was like as a young woman; was she hot? I tried to picture her thirty years earlier. I spied a little black and white picture of her with her arms around a short familiar-looking guy—Paul Simon, I think—and it confirmed my judgment. Even with big glasses, and a shape-hiding sweater, the young Rubenstein was totally hot.

She leaned forward. "Tony Beckwith says you've proposed a fascinating postdoc on prostitute imagery. He also tells me you're brilliant, but slow in getting started. He's also worried that you don't really know anything about prostitution. So I'm going to help you."

Dr. Rubenstein pushed back in her chair. I felt like an undergrad again as I tried to take down every word of her well-rehearsed speech about prostitution in New York City. She told me about the "sliding scale for sex acts" based on location: a blow job in lower Manhattan going for $200, while the same service in the Bronx might cost sixty dollars. She also noted a different sliding scale based on race. White and Asian prostitutes could charge twice as much as black women when the buyer was white, but even black men generally paid more for white prostitutes than for black prostitutes. She told me about the burgeoning business of prostitutes selling their services through Facebook and LinkedIn, and the battles being fought on reputable websites like Craigslist and Angie's List to keep prostitution off. She told me about common prostitute practices to increase safety, like never carrying cash and working in pairs. Finally, she talked about a Columbia University study that she supported. The study concluded that the average street-walking prostitute was physically abused four times a year; but escort-service prostitutes fewer times than once a year. The study also concluded that 50 percent of prostitutes work day jobs, generally service jobs like waitressing, and only hook part-time at night.

Then she spoke with me about her work in the School of Social Work with prostitutes and other at-risk women. She'd earned several grants for the university and had a small army of MSW students out on the streets distributing condoms and clean needles. She also initiated different support groups for the women trying to leave prostitution. I was a little annoyed by her PC terminology (i.e., *sex worker* instead of *prostitute*; *substance dependent* instead of *drug addict*) but bowled over by her mastery of the subject. After ten minutes, she paused.

"That was really helpful, Dr. Rubenstein."

She nodded as if my statement was obvious, but her facial expression was sympathetic. "So I'm supposed to help out by setting up a meeting between you and some sex workers. Is that about right, Dr. Hristahalios?"

I nodded.

"There're three women who visited my grad class a few weeks ago. These women are 'escorts,' not streetwalkers, and they provide services to white professional men. I think you will be more comfortable if you start your work with women like these—but I hope you'll understand that these women are not representative of the average woman who sells sex for money. And I think your research will be flawed if you confine your research to escorts and avoid streetwalkers—especially those women who sell their service in urban ghettos."

I nodded.

"The escorts will pick a place of their choice to meet you, probably near their clients in the East Village. You'll be expected to buy them dinner and a few drinks in exchange for their time. Don't keep them too long or they'll think you owe them more."

My heart started pounding with this news. I was grateful, but scared and could only sputter, "Thank you, thank you very much."

She smiled. "Dr. Hristahalios, I don't know you and I don't know if you've ever dealt with people like the women you'll be meeting. Understand that they are professionals—and their profession is built on extracting money from men to support themselves. This doesn't make them any worse than you or me, but they might meet you and, well, assume you're an easy target."

"Don't worry, Dr. Rubenstein, I'll be fine." It was unconvincing, but the best I could offer.

⁕

THE DETAILS from Rachel Rubenstein arrived via e-mail at noon the next day.

> You will be meeting three women who work under the names Monica, Alexandra, and Julia at a bar called the Buzz Kill at five this evening. The bar is on Avenue B in Alphabet City. They will expect dinner and a few drinks in exchange for the hour of speaking with you. They work at night, and begin working at six. So if you go longer than your hour, they will expect additional compensation. Good luck tonight. Rachel

I hadn't been to Alphabet City since first moving to New York seven years ago. But I remembered the neighborhood well. If the East Village is the low-rent cousin of Greenwich Village, then Alphabet City is the low-rent cousin of the East Village—a place for drifters, starving artists, and flamboyant alternative lifestyles. In the '60s, it was home to counterculture poets like Allen Ginsberg and the seminal punk band, The Fugs. It was the inspiration for District X, the impoverished ghetto inhabited by mutants in the *X-Men* comic books. More recently, it was the AIDS-ravaged setting for the musical *Rent* and Robert De Niro's grim art-house film, *Flawless*. Although gentrification is now making its mark on Alphabet City, it's still the roughest neighborhood in lower Manhattan.

When I first came to New York, I looked at some apartments in Alphabet City because they were cheap (at least by Manhattan standards) and within walking distance of NYU. The Drag Queens were a little too freaky for me, so I opted to pay more money and live farther away—renting a room in Brooklyn Heights, where I still live.

Coming out of the subway station at East Broadway, I was pleased to see that the neighborhood had cleaned up a bit. Many of the worst apartment buildings were demolished; others were refurbished, a couple even had doormen. But the progress was uneven, and I still had to step over a junkie as I came up onto the not-very crowded street. Even half-gentrified, this was still a nocturnal neighborhood that saved its color and characters for darkness.

The Buzz Kill was three blocks away. I entered the shuttered bar at 5:05. I was the only person in there other than a much-tattooed bartender. She looked up from her sci-fi paperback for just a split second as I entered. The place smelled like mildew and cigarettes, but the little table where I settled was clean and the vinyl upholstery in the booth mostly intact.

"You want something?" the bartender asked.

"Uh—I'm meeting some people here. Maybe just a Coke until then."

She read for another minute, then put down her book and brought over the soda. I took out my notebook, opened it to a clean page, and unclicked my pen. For the next ten minutes, I sipped my soda as slowly as I could. Finally, the silence was broken by the arrival of three women.

"Hi honey. You're the professor who's writing a book, right?" a slender dark-haired woman said as she slid into the booth across from me. "I'm Monica. So here's the thing, honey. We're businesswomen and we can talk to you until six if you buy us food and some cocktails from this fine establishment. That sound right to you, hon?"

"Yeah, uh, very right. I mean very good."

Two other women followed her. "Hi Professor, what's your name?" said a tall blonde woman now standing across from me.

"I'm Matthew Hristahalios. Matt is okay, if you don't mind."

"Sure. Like a welcome mat," giggled the blonde. "You can be our welcome Matt 'til six. Ain't that right? Scooch over, Mon, I'm coming in." The two women across from me both wore too much jewelry and tight outfits that displayed their nice figures. "I am Alexandra, and you met Monica. The redhead is Julia Roberts."

My head spun to the right to see Julia Roberts. She was standing over me, waiting to be seated on the booth bench. She was tall, shapely, auburn haired, slightly big mouthed, with a tight red halter top and tiny black miniskirt. She was straight out of *Pretty Woman*. Of course, she wasn't the real Julia Roberts—she was too young and not as leggy—but she was as close to the real thing as I'd ever seen.

I was paralyzed.

"Hey Professor, you gonna move so Julia can sit down?"

"Oh, why uh, um, sure."

Monica smiled knowingly. "Cat got your tongue, Professor?"

Julia Roberts looked at the bartender. "Hey, how about some hot wings and a pitcher of Red Death with four glasses?" Then she looked at me, "You ever drink Red Death, Professor?" She settled in next to me, pushing up against me as she came in.

I slid myself all the way to the wall to make room for her.

"It's all right. I don't bite—at least not too hard. Unless you like that kind of thing."

The girls laughed.

The bartender brought over a small pitcher filled with a dark pink punch and poured us four shots. We clinked glasses. Monica smiled, "So Professor, we're on the clock. What do you want to know?"

"Well, I have some interview questions in my bag . . ." I looked helplessly at my backpack, on the floor outside the booth on the other side of Julia Roberts. I briefly attempted to reach around her, brushing against her breasts as I did.

Julia smiled but didn't budge. I was stuck.

She took my pen and wrote on the top of the page: "Questions for New York's Top Three Hookers." Then she wrote on the page:

1. How long have you been hooking?

2. Why did you become a hooker?

3. What do you like best about hooking?

4. What do you like worst about hooking?

"Is anything in your bag really going to help you more than this, Professor?"

I took the pen from her. "You show the potential to be a fine qualitative researcher, Ms. Roberts. But I need to add one more question." I wrote, "Would you give up hooking if the right man came along and gave you a ticket out?"

Julia took the pen back from me, "I get that question a lot."

She put my notebook in front of her. "Pour another round, Professor. For the next forty minutes, you're my research assistant. Ms. Monica, Ms. Alexandra, the professor and I would like to ask you some questions. First, for background, how long you've been hooking?"

The next forty minutes were amazing. Over four pitchers of Red Death, three baskets of hot wings, and two baskets of jalapeno poppers, Julia Roberts interviewed her friends and they spoke candidly about themselves.

Monica was originally from Glens Falls in upstate New York. Her given name was Maria Dellasandro. She was from a strict Italian-Catholic family. She'd come to New York two years ago with hopes of making it as an actress; hooking paid the bills better than waitressing. She'd taken the name Monica for herself because she found a john with a thing for Courteney Cox, whom she vaguely resembled. It'd been six months since her last theatre audition and her waitressing was down to twice a week. Her john paid most of her bills. With the patronage of a good john, she was now okay with hooking, at least until she could figure out what to do with her life.

Alexandra was born in Kosovo, Yugoslavia, and was a child during that country's terrible civil war. Her family was sponsored by an evangelical church to come to the United States, and settled in rural Indiana. Her father hated living in the United States and never found steady work. He became an abusive alcoholic. Her mother worked two jobs to support the family. Alexandra ran away after her father brawled with her first boyfriend, but returned home a week later because she feared for her mother. She started hooking a little in Indiana to make some money, at least until her father found out. That night, he put her in the hospital with a broken chin. She'd been in New York for five years, four with the same escort service.

"They take $150 off the top. It's robbery, but I get set up with men who pay their bills. If he's a good man, I give him my panties with my name and e-mail at the end of the night so he'll remember me. I don't have a steady john like Mon, but I get plenty of repeats." Alexandra goes walking around Wall Street once or twice a week and stumbles into attractive men without wedding rings. She's actively dating and has not given up on "being a good wife and a good mother" at some point down the road.

Julia probed her friends and scribbled notes throughout, filling any white space left on the page with lovely swirls that turned into bird-like creatures. When Alexandra's story was done, Julia closed my notebook. "That's your hour, Professor. Thanks for the good time." She turned to the bartender, "Check please. Sugar Daddy will take this one."

Alexandra protested. "No, no, no. You little skunk, Julia, you never talk about yourself."

"Sorry, we're out of time. Time to get to work. What a shame." Julia slid toward the end of the booth. "Professor, you take the bill. We'll see you 'round." Monica and Alexandra stood up and walked toward the door. Julia took a couple of seconds to slide my pen into the spiral notebook and push it back to me. Then she stood up to follow her friends.

"No, stay Julia, I would like to know something about you, too." I reached over and touched her arm. "No, stay. Let's talk some more."

"You're sweet, Professor, but you're heading into john territory. See you later."

I pulled out my wallet. "Here. I have $200 in my wallet, and the check is only seventy-five dollars." I opened my wallet to show her the money, and placed the wallet on the table. "I still need to interview you. There's enough here for another pitcher of Red Death and basket of wings, and one hundred dollars for your pocket. Please stay."

She looked at Monica and Alexandra and laughed a little. Then she waved for them to go. She sat back down. "OK, but if you're giving me cash, that makes you a john. You got that?"

The words stung, but I took her hand and she sat back down. She took one hundred dollars out of my wallet. "You just got a hell of a lot cuter, Professor."

⁂

THREE HOURS later, I was bombed. The bar had filled up, and Julia and I ended up drinking with a gay male couple that asked to sit with us because there were no other seats. Much of that night is now blacked out from my memory. But I remember how it ended.

I remember Julia sitting on my lap and kissing her a little. The two of us pretended we were newlyweds from the Midwest, and we lied about our made-up lives to the bar's Bohemian clientele. After I ran out of money, Julia and I toasted our good future together, civil unions, and Truman Capote. Each time, the nice gay couple across from us bought us another round of drinks.

Then Julia kissed me on the mouth and excused herself for the bathroom. I hung around with my new friends for another half hour until they started asking about her. I poked my head into the women's bathroom. She was gone. I made up something about Julia recently losing a sister and still enduring bouts of needing to be alone.

I staggered out of the bar, onto the subway, and somehow made it home.

Conversation with Dad: September 9, 2012

I was watching a rerun of *Arrested Development*—great for recouping from a hangover because I know every line—when the phone rang. I thought about letting it ring into oblivion, then I muted the television and picked up the call.

"Hi, Dad."

"What makes you so sure it's me, Matty."

"Well, it's Sunday morning, so it's either you or the Lord. Between the two of you, you're the more reliable caller."

"Restrain your atheism, son. Bad enough I'm not in church myself right now. I don't need you runnin' down God when we talk. You have the whole week with your commie friends for that. Did you get my petition-of-the-week alert?"

"Is that the one from the Brothers of 'Nam?"

"Darn straight. Jack Greene wrote it a week ago after we talked at the VFW. We want the president to declare May 7 as Vietnam Veteran Recognition Day, to honor us vets for our service to our country. It's overdue. Sign our petition today."

"Glad you and your friends are being so productive."

"Is that a dig, son? I can't always tell with you." He paused, "So how you doin' with friends? Are you meeting anyone?"

Nothing made me more uncomfortable than Dad showing concern for my horrible social life—probably because his concerns were so well founded.

"Well, yeah, Dad, if you really want to know, I had a great time with three cute girls just last night. I even got a little friendly with one of them. A real 'looker' as you'd say."

"Hot damn, Matty, I'm so happy to hear this. Three of 'em? Heck, even in Vietnam, I never got more than two in one night. This makes my news for you even better."

"What's that, Dad?"

"Will Riley was by the other day. He needed to use the lift to switch out the tailpipe on his F-150. We started talking about you and he said he's been wanting to see you. He says he's always wanted to see New York, too. So I gave him your phone number and e-mail. He says he's going to get with Tim Dickey, square up some dates, and make plans to visit you. Great news, eh? Just be careful bringing these nice Midwestern boys out with your three fast New York City ladies. Okay?"

"Yeah, okay dad."

"You don't sound happy, Matt. What's up? Will and Tim are your best friends."

"No, Dad, this is great news. But I have to go now, I'm just feeling a little sick. That's all." At least that much of the conversation wasn't a lie.

CHAPTER 4

Wee Willy and Tiny Tim

Just as Dad promised, Will e-mailed me that evening. I reluctantly opened the e-mail:

Dude,

You've been hidin' long enough—gone to New York City to be a hermit. Aint right. So me and Tim are gonna flush you out. Two country-boys gonna take New York next weekend. Unbolt the liquor cabinet and unleash the girls. Should be there on Friday. What the hell's your address anyway? Call me at xxx—xxx—xxxx.

I had no beef with Will and Tim. They were my best friends in high school, where we played football and wrestled together. But it had been five years since I'd been back in Morris—and that was for Mom's funeral. It was hardly the week for getting silly with old friends. I graduated from college seven years ago. That was the last time I had shared a laugh with either of them.

Through occasional e-mails and updates from Dad, I knew that both Will and Tim were still in Morris. Will was working for his dad in the family business, the "1-2-Tree Lumberyard" on the edge of town, and he did odd jobs for Dad on weekends, usually driving across the upper Midwest in search of hard-to-find truck parts. Tim now worked as an assistant manager at the supermarket where he had worked ever since high school. They were both good guys but neither had ever lived outside Morris or dated a girl from outside of Grundy County. They likely never would. I wasn't like them any more, if I ever was.

But I couldn't blow them off. With trepidation, I called Will and firmed up plans for their visit.

○═╪═○

MOST OF the week was lost to fretting about the details of their visit. On the upside, it forced me to catch up on some long overdue chores: dusting the apartment, throwing out old clothes that I was now too fat to wear, and getting something into the refrigerator besides leftover General Tso's Chicken and Vitamin Water. While doing this, I rediscovered two lost items of some sentimental value. The first was an award from NYU for graduating with a 4.0 GPA from my master's program; the second was a picture of Mom smoking a joint with a black guy in Washington Square Park. It was taken the year before her death during her only visit to New York. Dad didn't come—and Mom was unbridled that week. There's nothing weirder than having to reign in your mother. It might have been the only time I ever saw her truly happy.

Academically, the week was lost. I couldn't concentrate on anything. When I wasn't fretting about Will and Tim's visit, I was thinking about that night of fooling around with Julia Roberts. But I did manage to type up a padded weekly progress report and attached Julia's excellent notes from the interviews with her friends. I sent these two files to Dr. Beckwith along with a first draft of the interview protocol. This created the appearance of scholarly momentum and kept him off my back.

As the day of Will and Tim's arrival came closer, I became more focused on my responsibilities to show them a good time. It would be their first—and likely only—visit to New York City. As kids, we'd grown up two hours from Chicago, and visited it a few times. We did all the regular tourist things. But neither Will nor Tim ever went to Chicago anymore. They were twenty-eight and single (Tim had already married and divorced). We all understood that they weren't coming to New York City to see the Statue of Liberty—unless it entailed looking up her gown to see if she shaves her private parts.

I knew nothing about carousing in New York, so I did what any introverted New Yorker would do under these circumstances; I went on the Internet and typed "best places for singles in Manhattan." I made a list of bars and resolved to check out a few of them.

One was a bar in the East Village called the Blue Owl Lounge. I dropped by that Thursday evening at nine. I ordered a beer and looked around the half-filled, blue-lit bar. I clapped halfheartedly when the smooth jazz guitarist—well practiced in the art of sounding indifferent to his art—finished his set. Then my jaw dropped; there was Julia Roberts with some guy who looked as old as Dad.

Intellectually, I knew I had no claim on Julia Roberts. I knew she was a hooker and she sold herself to whichever guy financed the particular night out. That's how the profession works. But I was still angry with her and even angrier with myself for feeling jealous. From a distance, I watched her whisper into the old guy's ear, laughing at his every reply.

I moved a little closer and sat down directly in back of her so she couldn't see me. I watched her whisper into the old guy's ear, giggle at his whispers, and lean in for kisses—just as she had with me a week earlier.

When she got up to go to the bathroom, I followed her right in.

Like all Manhattan bathrooms, the women's room at the Blue Owl is tiny. We were only three feet away from each other—which seemed to have surprised me more than her. I trembled as I brushed against her arm.

Julia grinned, as if expecting to see me. She spoke casually, "Oh, hey, Professor. Whoa—I guess you got a kinky stalker thing for me going on now. You should write a paper about that."

Her sarcasm stung and I stepped backward before regaining some composure. "No, uh, don't be crazy. Strictly business, Julia."

"So what's your business in the ladies' room?"

"Well, I have two old friends coming into town this weekend." I tried sounding smooth. "So, you know, I think it would be cool if, well, maybe you and me, and Monica and Alexandra, could meet and hang out. Not like in a sexual way. Just meet and hang together. You know what I mean?"

"Yeah, hang together. I do a lot of hanging, Professor. How much money you got? I could show your friends a really good time, or a not-so-good time. It just kinda depends."

"Well, um, again, I don't mean to buy sex. And I am a postdoc; it's not like I'm made of money. I'll bet your income is greater than mine. But you and your friends are fun and my friends are fun and I think we could have fun, you know, together—over dinner and drinks. And I could, you know, help you and your friends with some of the expenses of meeting us for the night, if you know what I mean. Like transportation and, um, well, other miscellaneous expenses."

"Miscellaneous expenses? Oh, sure I got lots of them. I don't know, Professor, playing dating games with little boys doesn't get my rent paid. Monica's got a steady john on the weekends—it'd take a lot for her to cancel on him. Alexandra usually has a date. But let me talk to some people I know. Maybe we could work something out. You're a sweet guy and I don't meet that many sweet guys. Write your phone number on this paper and I'll give you a call." I did and she kissed me on the lips, but only for a second.

"They're coming tomorrow afternoon. Let me know soon, okay?"

But she was gone. I stood alone in the women's room of a singles bar wondering if I had just made a terrible mistake.

FRIDAY AT noon, my phone rang. I let it ring to voicemail, then played the message. "Matt-lock, it's Will. How you doin', man? We're on Route 78, just crossed into Jersey. Will see you at Newark Liberty Airport in an hour." The last thing I needed was Will's jacked-up redneck truck parallel parking on the jammed, narrow streets of Brooklyn Heights. So I told him I would meet him at Newark airport and bring him and Tim over by train.

I took the subway into Manhattan and jumped onto the PATH train to the airport. Coming out of the tube, I double-checked my phone to see if Julia had called. Nothing. "A prostitute is late checking in with an impoverished client. Now there's a surprise. I'll never hear from her." I cursed myself for suggesting I didn't have a lot of money—kiss of death to a hooker.

I met my old friends without a hitch. It was the middle of the day, so the station was mostly empty. They smiled stupidly as I walked toward them. While I had misgivings about the visit, seeing those two goofy grins on those homely faces made me feel good for the first time in weeks.

The moment didn't last. Before I even reached them, Tim called out: "Dude. You got really fat. Not enough double frogging, I bet."

Great. Not even a minute into our visit and the story of "double frog" was already being thrown in my face. "Double frog" was the nickname that followed me through childhood. I was christened with it at age ten when I came out of the swamp behind Dad's house and explained to my friends that I had just seen this amazing animal—a "double frog." My friends, more savvy than I because of older siblings or parents who talked about sex in the house, laughed at me for my double frog sighting, and kept laughing about it for the next ten years. Word spread, and I was called "the double frog boy" all through high school. My only real date in four years of high school—a night at the movies with Vicki Werner—was broken up with shouts about double frog and loud croaking sounds that built toward orgasm. Vicki, desperate to attain popular-crowd status, quickly realized that being seen with the double frog boy was bad for her image. She never made the same mistake again. Neither did any other girl from Morris High School.

Seeing the discomfort on my face from being greeted with "double frog," Will corrected. "Not cool. Matt, forgive Tim, the long ride has left him with Tourette's. Tim, try this: Matt, it's great to see you, my man." Then he winked, "And congratulations on the baby."

The idiots punched each other in the arm and, after a couple of perfunctory man hugs, we were on the train back into the city.

On the train, we talked about what to do for the weekend. I gave them a bunch of choices: walking downtown past Ground Zero, taking the ferry to Ellis Island and the Statue of Liberty, or walking midtown from the Empire State Building to Times Square. I mentioned the museums and the aquarium. I even gave them a few unusual suggestions that I picked up from the Internet: kayaking the Hudson River, the Seinfeld Reality Tour, a backstage tour of Radio City Music Hall. They nodded through each of these.

"This stuff is fine, Dude, but we really want to just hang with you. It's been way too long. We miss you, man," Will finally said. "We came here for you, not for the Statue of Liberty. You can get rid of Morris, but you can't get rid of us."

Tim ended the warm and fuzzy moment. "Yeah, and your dad told Will that you've landed some fine tail. Maybe you can fix us up with some city girls while we're here. These poor girls don't see a lot of real men. It would be good for them to taste some country sausage."

I looked at my cell phone; there were no messages.

I SHOWED my friends the best time I could. I gave them a tour of Brooklyn Heights, walking the promenade on the East River with its magnificent views of Manhattan. I wended us through blocks with 150-year-old row homes, and told my friends about the many famous people who had lived in Brooklyn Heights over the years. I rattled off the names of the great American authors who'd lived here: Truman Capote, Norman Mailer, Arthur Miller, Tom Wolfe, and Andrea Dworkin. Despite his redneck exterior, Will reads good fiction, and he liked walking in the shadows of so many famous authors. Tim looked bored. The only name that got a small rise out of him was Adam Yauch, founder of the Beastie Boys.

We kayaked the Hudson River. They nearly died when I took them to the Carnegie Deli and the waiter brought out sandwiches the size of a human head. They kidded me about all the academic awards I had won in high school without ever really studying. We relived the time I won the county's student poetry contest by submitting some lyrics from a forgotten Meat Loaf comeback album. We sang the last two lines of the song together:

> Behind every man who has somethin' to say,
> There's a boy who had nothin' to lose
> An' every hero was once, every villain was once,
> just a boy with a bad attitude

Yes, we had some nostalgic laughs. And my old friends didn't press me when I failed to produce a single friend, male or female. But the trip was dull. The highlight was probably Harpo, who miraculously started singing "birds can't talk" on cue with their arrival. We howled every time Harpo belted it out.

SATURDAY WAS much the same, a couple of perfectly pleasant activities, but nothing that two young men looking for a wild weekend would consider memorable. The weekend was going okay, but I was hardly showing them a great time.

It was eleven on Saturday night. I was walking Will and Tim back to my apartment when my phone buzzed. I looked at the display to see I was being called from a phone number called "UNKNOWN CALLER." I picked up, "Professor? Is this Professor Welcome Matt!?!?" There was noise and laughter in the background. "It's Julia. Wanna party?"

"Sure, babe. I always wanna party with you," I said into the phone trying to sound cool to my friends, and trying to conceal my excitement at this amazing turn of events. I saw big, dopey grins on Will and Tim's faces as they heard me cement the details with Julia about meeting at my place.

We bought some liquor and headed back to my apartment. Will, always a goofball, went into my closet and put on a blue-and-red-striped tie—which went appallingly with his brown flannel shirt. Tim fussed with his hair a little, seeking to cover his emerging bald spot. I sat on the edge of my bed fretting over how to break the ice when the girls arrived and not coming up with a single good idea.

I buzzed up Julia a half hour later. She came with two friends, neither of whom I had seen before. One had a nice, thin body, like Julia, but her face was messed up on one side—perhaps from a burn. The other one was too heavy for decent hooking I imagine, but not quite fat enough to be called fat. Neither was top shelf, or even second shelf, but I was happy for anything at this point.

Entering the apartment, Julia put her arms around me and gave me a long, delicious kiss. I grew a giant erection. She tasted almost metallic, and my tongue tingled and burned a little. I now understand it was from cocaine residue. But I didn't care at the time—at least not much. A beautiful woman had just given me a giant kiss in front of my two friends. Even if she left now, the weekend was redeemed.

Julia pulled me out into the stairwell landing as her friends entered. "So, here's the deal, Professor. You couldn't afford me, Monica and Alexandra tonight. Trust me on that. But I'll play like I'm your adorable girlfriend and my two, um, colleagues will show your goober friends a good time. It's $400 for the night and this includes me taking care of my friends. Any sex is extra—if you don't want it, don't do it. All regular charges apply. Sound good to you, honey?" Then she looked down at my pants and touched my erection. "But because you're so happy to see me . . . I'll get you off right now in this stairway. That's a freebie because I've got a great buzz and you look so cute and clueless."

She dropped to her knees and opened my pants. Her mouth was on my erection before I could stop her. But I did, by stumbling and falling backward into the apartment with my pants down. Julia tumbled into the apartment too, right on top of me, her skirt flipped upward revealing her red bikini panties. Everyone erupted in deafening laughter.

For maybe an hour, we drank screwdrivers and close-danced to R&B music from Julia's iPod. Then Julia and her friends disappeared into my tiny bathroom—I never would have guessed it could hold three people. Will and Tim argued briefly over who would get stuck with the fat chick. After flipping a coin, Tim backslapped his friend, "Chin up, Willy, the more the cushin', the better the pushin'." The girls emerged half-dressed and giggly.

The drinks kept coming. We told the girls a few stories about Morris. Tim told everyone the story of me and the double frog and everyone laughed at my expense. Julia sat in my lap and purred, "Well, you can double frog me 'til your head explodes, Professor."

We paired up throughout my one-and-a-half-room apartment. Julia's friends talked dirty, in stupid phrases that I thought were only spoken in porn movies. They taunted Will and Tim for "being country boys with little peckers" and called my friends "Wee Willy and Tiny Tim." Will and Tim responded by playfully wrestling with the girls, slapping their rumps, and shouting out "double frog" as the wrestling progressed into sex. We bedded down in three pairs: Julia and me on my bed; Tim and burn-face on my futon sofa; Will and the heavy girl on an air mattress on the kitchen floor.

Drunk and happy, I watched Julia undress me. I put my hands on her breasts and she rubbed my penis. She put a condom on my erection and climbed on top. We grunted and croaked together until it was over—twenty seconds later.

I whispered to her, "I'm sorry, that probably wasn't much fun for you."

She whispered back, "It's okay, honey. This is business. And it's sweet that you cared enough to ask."

It took twenty-eight years, but I finally had been inside a woman. I fell into a deep sleep.

Sometime later, I was awakened by jostling next to my bed. Burn-face was pawing through my dresser. The lights were still on in the apartment and I squinted at her rough, yellowish skin. She looked at me, smiled and whispered, "Hey Babe, you got my money?"

I reached out my arm to pat Julia awake. My arm landed on the mattress. I sat up. She was gone. I dropped my hand to the floor and grabbed my pants. I pulled out my wallet and opened it. It was empty.

"Fuck. She robbed me," I whispered. "Where'd Julia go? She has my money."

Burn-face shrugged, "Don't know, Babe, but where's my fifty bucks. I get mine now and I'm gone. If I don't, I can be a world of trouble for you in this nice Brooklyn Heights row house."

"Keep your pants on." I stood up and walked across the room—three whole steps—to the mantle that doubled as my entertainment center. I opened the little jar where my research funds were kept and pulled out fifty dollars. I gave it to burn-face. She smiled and then pointed to her friend, still sleeping on the kitchen floor with Will. "And hers, too. Hon?" I took out another fifty dollars.

She slapped her friend's foot. Heavy-girl sat up. They dressed quickly. Heavy-girl spoke quietly, "Good-bye Wee Willy. Good-bye Tiny Tim. Good-bye Professor. Don't worry 'bout Julia, Baby, she likes you. But she never spends the whole night anywhere." I locked the door as they exited.

THE NEXT morning, Sunday, I roused my friends and fed them freshly squeezed orange juice from the local bodega—now owned by Koreans—and fresh bagels from the local Jewish bakery, also now owned by Koreans. One of Tim's remarks summed up the visit in their estimation: "Matty, you've gone from super douche to super dude. Those chicks were crazy. Not beautiful, but crazy. And they kicked themselves out of bed. We don't even have to pretend we'll call. You're the king."

"And your girlfriend, Julia, is one amazing girl," Will offered. "We don't have girls like that in Morris. Now I know why you never come home. She's Girls-Gone-Wild caliber."

We rode the train out to Newark airport together and said our good-byes.

Conversation with Dad: September 23, 2012

Dad didn't call the weekend of September 15, knowing Will and Tim were visiting. His next call came reliably at 10 A.M. the following Sunday.

"Hey, Matty. It's Dad."

"I know. Hi, Dad."

"How was your visit last week?"

"Fine."

"Come on, Matty. You can do better than that."

"Um, it was, um, good, Dad. What do you want to know?"

"Well, you can start by talking to your father. You don't get a lot of visitors, and you've never been visited by your best friends from Morris. Tell me about their visit."

"Geez, Dad, don't get upset. It was a nice visit. I took them kayaking in the Hudson and then to the Carnegie Deli on Friday. On Saturday we walked the Brooklyn Bridge into Manhattan and went to Chinatown for lunch. We had a few drinks on Saturday night, and then they went home on Sunday. It was a nice weekend."

"And?"

"And what, Dad?"

"And I think you can tell your father about this girlfriend of yours. Why do I have to learn about her from Will?"

"What'd he tell you?"

"Not much, only that she's tall and pretty. I don't pry Matt, but I wish you'd talk to me."

"Well, um, she's—a real fun New York girl. Not like the girls back home. But we're not real serious, Dad." I blushed. Conning my friends was one thing, but I felt dirty lying to my father.

"What's her name?"

"Julia, um, Julia Roberts-son. Julia Robertson is her name."

"Sounds like a nice name. I'm glad you have someone. Your mother and I worried so much when you went through high school and then college without a girlfriend. Do you remember when I got Jeff Storer's niece to be your prom date because you were too nervous to ask anyone?"

"Yes, I remember that. And thanks so much for reminding me about that wonderful moment in my life."

"Well, I don't mean to embarrass you. Just promise me that if you and this Robertson girl get serious, you'll tell me. Okay?"

"Okay, Dad, but honestly, I don't think Julia is the kind of girl who gets serious with her boyfriends."

"Boyfriends? Tell me if I'm stepping over the line, but your girlfriend's not the kind of girl who sleeps around, is she?"

"I think that is over the line, as a matter of fact." I did my best to sound offended. "I'm changing the subject. I saw your petition-of-the-week e-mail—trying to get Pete Rose into the baseball Hall of Fame? Why do you care?"

"I care because he's the game's greatest hitter—even if he's not a choir boy. It's nobody's business, really, if he did some ugly things off the field."

Dad's comments made me feel better about Julia. If she is making people happy, what'd it matter if she was hooking?

"I'll sign that petition. Bye, Dad. I'll call you in a week."

CHAPTER 5

Betting on the Cum

I was now cover boy for *Living-a-Lie Illustrated*: I lied to my father about having a real girlfriend; I conned my old friends into thinking I was a dude with fun friends; and I pulled this off by financing sexual favors, including the loss of my own virginity, with the center's research funds. I also was attempting to con the center's faculty into believing I was making progress on my research, when all I was doing was procrastinating and misspending their money.

That next Tuesday, Dr. Beckwith asked me and Randy Skiles to meet him for a lunch at a little Chinese place a few blocks from the center on Eleventh Avenue. Over a steaming bowl of soupy dumplings, Beckwith told us about the owner, a Chinese man born in Vietnam. The owner fled Vietnam when Saigon fell. He came to the United States as a refugee. "Most Americans don't realize this," he said between slurps of brown broth, "but there're Chinese enclaves all across Asia. The Chinese merchant class spread its wings like the Jews spread across Europe."

"Yes, Dr. Beckwith, but I more liken the Chinese diaspora across Asia to the Indian diaspora across the British colonial empire. Unlike the Jews but like the Indians, the Chinese emigres were deliberately transplanted by a colonizing empire to provide a trustworthy managerial class in their colonial outposts." Randy Skiles spoke with the confidence of a fine charlatan: knowing just enough to present plausible conjecture as fact.

"That's wonderful, Randy. Your grounding in the cross-cultural migrations forced by colonialism will serve you well when you interview for faculty jobs next year." Beckwith slurped down another dumpling.

A plate of eggplant and green peppers, along with three rice bowls, arrived at the table. I've never liked eggplant much, but I wasn't going to make a fuss.

"The eggplant looks magnificent!" Randy brownnosed. "The Asian variety has just a little bit more of a garlicky taste than the European."

Beckwith and Randy attacked the plate with their chopsticks, picking up and dropping off vegetable pieces on top of their rice. I waited.

"Oh, pardon me, Matthew, I didn't know you were uncomfortable with chopsticks." Beckwith raised his hand for the waiter.

"Allow me." Randy turned toward the waiter and spoke. "我能为我的朋友斩棒吗?" He turned back toward us. "I only know a little Cantonese, but fortunately, this is something I can handle."

The waiter promptly brought me a fork.

"Bravo, Randy," Beckwith smiled.

For the next few minutes the three of us said more wonderful things about eggplant. A big bowl of rice porridge with pieces of a yellowy meat came next. I wished for a burger as my teeth wrestled with the rubbery pieces. I nearly gagged when Beckwith asked me if I had eaten intestine before.

"So, gentlemen, wonderful food aside, let's hear about your work. While I chair your committees, today we are colleagues interested only in supporting each other. So please be candid in discussing the challenges you're experiencing, and we'll be equally candid in the feedback we offer each other. We are a team committed to each other's success. Right?" Beckwith looked at me.

"Of course."

"Good. Matthew, let's focus on your project first since, I think it's fair to say, you've been a little slower to get everything pulled together for IRB. Randy cleared IRB last week."

For the next twenty minutes, I was pummeled in the kindest and most analytic academic language possible. Beckwith brought a copy of the interview protocol I e-mailed him a week earlier. We dissected it and rewrote it together right there amidst the tripe and eggplant. Randy offered a few helpful suggestions, but they were bracketed in condescension with statements like, "This is a fine starting point, but still rough" and "I understand why you wrote this, but I don't think it's field ready yet."

When the protocol was rewritten, Beckwith said: "Thanks, gentlemen, this is the kind of collaboration that assures mutual success. Randy, at some point, I am sure Matthew will help you too. I hope you'll seek him out."

Then Beckwith turned to me: "Matthew. Test this with a few of your subjects this week and make sure it yields the kind of feedback you need. Forward the protocol with notes from your test interviews and a sampling plan to me by week's end. I will send it along to the IRB on Monday, okay?"

"Certainly, Dr. Beckwith."

Beckwith rose, dropped twenty dollars on the table, and left.

Once Beckwith cleared the restaurant's door, I did the same, leaving Randy with forty dollars and a nod.

ALTHOUGH IT was done politely, there was no mistaking that Beckwith had just given me a dope-slap. I had a track record of starting slowly, so I wasn't all that worried. But Beckwith was my funding source, and he was nervous about my slow start. If his nervousness progressed into disaffection, he could petition the committee to suspend my funding. I recalled the two paragraphs at the back of the fellowship award letter—broadly written language reserving the right of the committee chair, more or less, to curtail the fellowship or place the fellow on supervised probation at his discretion. I hadn't done any real work in the month since the fellowship officially began, so I was vulnerable if Beckwith were inclined to move against me.

I needed to contact Julia Roberts. She'd be my gateway to other prostitutes and she also owed me the hundred dollars I pulled from my research kitty. But I had no way to get in touch with her—her cell phone showed as 'unknown caller' and I had no idea where she lived. I'd have to see Rachel Rubenstein again.

I headed east toward the main campus. As luck would have it, I reached the academic building's lobby as Rachel was leaving. She was in a hurry so she asked me to walk with her to the subway.

Bobbing between people on the crowded sidewalk, I attempted to stay next to her. "Dr. Rubenstein, it might not be something you usually do, but I need the phone number of Julia Roberts. She's become important to my research."

She stopped. "No. These women trust me because I don't give out their contact information. You might understand that some men—even scholars—harbor complicated feelings toward these women because of the services they deliver. Sex workers often don't want to be recontacted after a business transaction—and your interview with Ms. Roberts and her friends was just that, a business transaction. It was completed. If Ms. Roberts chose not to give you her contact information, I don't think I can either."

Inside, I was wild at the thought of not getting to Julia Roberts again, but I tried to stay cool. "Well, Rachel, I understand your caution and applaud your concern for these women. But Julia Roberts helped me finalize the interview questions and showed a genuine interest in the project. I believe she'd want to participate again."

We paused at the subway entrance. Rubenstein looked at me as a puff of warm, smelly air rose up from the tube and blew her graying long hair all about her head: "Here's what I can do. I will e-mail her and encourage her to contact you. Give me your number. Then it will be her choice." She took out a business card and handed me the blank side.

"But Matthew, I will not do this for you again. These women direct their own affairs. I am not Ms. Roberts's agent and you are not one of her johns. I know your interest in seeing Ms. Roberts again is *solely* professional. That's right, isn't it?"

"Of course, Rachel." I tried to sound convincing. I wrote down my phone number and passed the card back to her.

"Of course," she repeated as she descended into the subway.

At eleven fifteen the next night, while watching two hot chicks wrestle on YouTube, I received a text message from 'unknown caller': "this is JR. what u want?"

My heart skipped a beat. I texted right back: "i want 2 C U"

"y"

"work. need 2 interview 5 hookers."

"y u need me?"

"u get me 2 them. i pay u."

"i will c. gtg."

And that was it. She was gone.

I HEARD nothing more from Julia until Thursday at nine fifteen P.M. I was desperate when her text came in; I needed to finalize and test the protocol for Beckwith by Friday. The text message arrived from the now familiar 'unknown caller.'

"Cum to 277 Ave C, 5C. U can speak to 5 like me. $40 each 4 them. $50 2 me. Cum now."

I didn't like having terms dictated through a text message, but this was my only chance. I needed to conduct the test interviews; and I needed to see Julia. She owed me money and I wanted to kiss her again.

"On my way. What's your number?" I texted.

"Y"

"Might get lost."

"U R smart. Don't get lost."

"Ok. But I might."

"Fine. 718-764-3069. I don't give it out. Don't burn me."

I CAME up from the subway in the East Village and walked into Alphabet City. It was easy to find the apartment building, a recently refurbished tenement from the 1920s. I spoke "This is Julia's friend" into the intercom and was buzzed into the lobby.

I got off the elevator on the fifth floor and walked down a narrow hallway to apartment 5C. The door was unlocked and I entered. The apartment was hot and smelled of sweat. Six women and a skinny man were sitting around a bridge table, playing cards. Loud guitar music—was it *Guns N' Roses?*—was playing.

Coming closer, I could see they were playing poker—a cash game. I saw a half-empty vodka bottle and two empty wine bottles. A mirror with two rolled-up dollar bills told me that they'd been snorting coke.

I didn't recognize the women, and, at first, even missed Julia who was in a hoodie and jeans—casual attire for a hooker on her night off. But coming closer, her auburn hair and tall stature pulled my eyes toward her. When she saw me, she stood up. "This is that nice professor I was telling you about. He wants to talk to us about sex-working."

She motioned to a folding chair, "Join us."

I grabbed the chair and wedged it between Julia and a young olive-skinned girl. I wondered if she was Mexican, Greek or Mideastern. She smiled, "Do you like what you see, Professor? Give me a half hour to take these girls to the cleaners, and then I'm all yours for $200."

"Oh no, Gabi. The professor's just here for research." The girls laughed. I blushed.

Julia finally spoke, "Hon, before you get too comfortable and start your interviews, there's the matter of my fifty dollars."

"Julia, um-in my way of—uh—thinking, you owe me a hundred dollars from the other night. So, just give—um—give me fifty dollars and, well, that will work fine."

A hard look came over Julia's face. "Holy shit, Professor. You're a cheap bastard, aren't you? We had some fun together. You were stiff the whole time; why's that, if you weren't into it? I don't remember you screaming rape. You think it was free?" She lowered her voice. "No, Professor, you pay for the services you receive."

"I didn't ask for any service from you. I was drunk. You practically forced yourself on me."

The table erupted in giggles; the skinny guy's high-pitched laugh was loudest of all. It was apparent that I would get no money from Julia. They continued with their poker game as if I weren't even there.

The girls started telling stories about welching johns. Julia poured me a screwdriver, which I drank as I listened to them describe their sad and funny stories about pathetic men.

After a few minutes of this, the olive-skinned girl leaned into my ear and whispered. "If you want to stay, you have to pay. Julia likes you or you wouldn't be here. But you still have to pay. You don't want to have to tell your professor friends that you got your ass kicked by six working girls." Then she blew gently in my ear and ran her tongue around the edge. I grew an erection.

I thought about protesting again, but it was clear that, short of grabbing a hundred dollars off the table and running for the door, I was out the money. I still needed to test the protocol. I was beaten.

I opened my wallet and took out $300. Julia pulled the money from my hands and gave two twenties to each of her five friends, even the skinny guy, and took fifty dollars for herself.

"That leaves you fifty dollars for poker, Professor. Have another drink and we'll talk over cards."

And so it went. I took out the protocol and interviewed each of the girls between hands of Texas hold'em and a silly, eight-card game they played called "Screw Your Neighbor."

The apartment was hot, the screwdrivers icy, and the well-lubricated girls spoke freely. Although Dr. Beckwith would wince at the forum in which I was conducting the interviews, I was getting honest feedback from six prostitutes (one a gay male). The fact that Julia deflected the questions to her friends and never talked about herself was not lost on me. But I let it go because I was getting great material from the other girls.

By one, I had five interviews completed and a fabulous buzz. The drinks and the distraction of the interviews resulted in some poor card playing. After winning a few hands early, I kept four cards and drew one, tossing in money as two girls bet aggressively against me. One of the girls speculated that I was chasing a flush. There were giggles about me "betting on the come" and also "betting on my cum later on."

As any poker player would have predicted, the flush never materialized. I lost all of my hard-won $120 on that one hand.

A little drunk and very tired, I pushed back from the table, tipped over the folding chair, and flopped on the couch. I tried to look pitiful, hoping Julia or one of the other girls would come over and sit with me. They ignored me. I dozed off.

I WOKE up once during the night, but after a disoriented minute, the alcohol put me back down. At five forty-five, I awoke again with a stiff neck and a piss erection. I wandered into the bathroom, peeking into the apartment's two bedrooms on my way. Four girls were sleeping in the rooms, but Julia was gone. My head hurt—it was the beginning of what promised to be a wretched hangover.

I peed, washed my hands, splashed water on my face, and went into the kitchen. I rinsed a mostly empty Pepsi bottle, filled it with cool water, and left the apartment. Then, I remembered what a proper male guest in a woman's apartment must do before leaving. I returned to the bathroom and lowered the toilet seat.

An hour later, I was back in my bed. Sometime around seven, I fell back asleep.

Conversation with Dad: September 28, 2012

The phone rang later that morning, and kept ringing. It shook me out of the sleep I had started only three hours earlier. I peeked at the clock: ten fifteen. The sleep hadn't rested me much, but had allowed my brain to fully dehydrate. A massive hangover surged forward to the front of my head as I lifted myself up to grab the phone.

"Yes," I groaned.

"Geez, Matty, you sound horrible. A wild night at some bar with that girlfriend of yours, I bet?"

"Something like that."

"Well, then you'll love my newest petition. I'm telling Governor Quinn to stop trying to solve the government's problems by overtaxing drinks. It ain't fair and the governor keeps talking about more gas and booze taxes. I'm sending the petition today and am pushing for a last wave of signatures. That's why I'm calling you early this week."

"Cheap booze for our drunks and cheap gas for our SUVs. Sounds great," I groaned.

"Can you give me something better than mumbles? Jeez, I can barely hear you."

I cradled the phone between ear and shoulder and grabbed the Advil off the top of the upturned milk crate that doubled as my nightstand. I swallowed two little brown pills and slipped the phone back into my hand. Pleased by my minor gymnastic success, my guard came down.

"Yeah, sorry Dad. It's more than me sleeping off a rough night. It's been a very hard week."

"What's up, buddy?"

"It's hard to fully explain, Dad. But, like so many things in life, it comes down to money. Having a girlfriend is expensive; pushing forward on my research with prostitutes is expensive; living in New York is expensive. Everything is expensive. My fellowship stipend and research allocation can't cover it all."

"You mean to tell me that they're not paying you a ton of money to interview hookers? There's a shocker," Dad snickered. Then his conscience caught up with him.

"Matty, I'm not a rich man. You know that. But the shop is doing better now, and I have some money put away for you. You know it's for when you get married and want to buy a house and give me some grandkids. I could release some of that money to you a little early. But before I do, you're going to need to do some things."

"What's that, Dad?" I braced for a lecture.

"First, you need to get a real job. I don't know how hard you're workin' on this fellowship, but I bet it's not so much that you can't tend bar on the weekend or wait tables a few nights a week. Second, I think you need to look at how you're spending money with this girlfriend of yours. Is she paying her freight? If this girl really likes you, she don't need you takin' her out all the time. And, third, this research of yours—you better be watching yourself with these hookers. They're smart and they're good at taking a young man's money."

Dad's voice amped up a little. "Matty, you been livin' away from home for seven years. This is the first time you've complained about money. And it's just a few weeks after you started talkin' with hookers. I'm bettin' that's not a coincidence. So, if you want some money from dear old Dad, you gotta come home for it. I'll pay your plane fare. Spend a week at home; bring this girlfriend of yours. I'd like to meet her. Hell, it's been five years since you've come home, and that was only for your mother's funeral. I think it'd be good for you to spend a week back here in America, away from all those professors and hookers."

"I can't go home now, Dad. It's the middle of the semester and I'm in the middle of my research. I'm sorry I told you that I was low on money."

"Me too, Sonny Boy."

"Bye, Dad."

Chapter 6

Linner with My Frenemy

Monday went well. I presented the protocol and preliminary interview results to all three members of my committee: Drs. Beckwith, Peck, and Banjari, and Randy Skiles. Nobody gave me a bad time for being late on the submission. However, predictably, Randy was a pompous ass. Throughout my presentation, he offered faint praise, but it was obvious to me that he was trying to trip me up. Here were two of his questions:

"Matthew, this is interesting preliminary work, but how will it stand up to diversity challenges? Do you plan to get beyond prostitutes who appear to cater to straight, white men? How are you sure you're engaging a representative sample of sex workers?"

"I am intrigued by your line of inquiry Matthew, but how do you control for a capitalist-tinged version of the Hawthorne effect? Specifically, does underwriting these women, however small the remuneration, bias them toward giving you answers they perceive you want to hear?"

But I finally had weaseled my way past the committee and had real preliminary findings. Not even Randy's veiled snark could hold me back. When the presentation was done, Beckwith affirmed the day's success: "Good, please prepare your final IRB package. I will make sure it gets in front of the board on Thursday." He gave me a pat on the back as I stood up to leave the center's basement meeting room.

Exiting the center, I heard Randy calling from behind, "Wait. WAIT."

I debated ignoring him but slowed my walk to let Randy catch up. I sensed him coming up behind me. "Hristahalios, I mean Matthew. I feel like we have not gotten off on the right foot. As the two 2013 fellows we should be great resources to each other, friendly at least, if not necessarily friends. Don't you agree?"

"Sure, Randy. I thought we were great chums. Thanks for lobbing me those softballs in front of the committee."

"Oh, I'm sorry. But don't take my questions the wrong way. I like what you're doing. I cannot keep myself from asking tough questions; your work interests me. If I were disdainful of it, I would have been silent."

"Disdain is a greatly undervalued trait."

"Oh, you are funny." He smiled. Reluctantly, I did too.

"Please, Matthew. You misunderstand me. And that is my fault. Let's hit the reset button on our relationship. Maybe we can take dinner together? I remember from our meeting with Dr. Beckwith a week ago that you like to walk across the Brooklyn Bridge into Chinatown. How about meeting in Chinatown this Friday? We could meet on the early side, before all the baronets of Wall Street descend on it?"

"Fine, Randy but don't order a bunch of pretentious stuff. I like General Tso and fried rice—Chinese KFC with mashed potatoes."

Randy grimaced but quickly changed his expression back to neutral. "That's fine, Matthew, whatever you'd like. I would like to bring my fiancée, Suzanne Ronkin. You will like her; she's an archivist at the New York Historical Society. A real New Yorker, full of stories about her city. That is, of course, if you have someone you'd like to bring as well?" He took out his wallet and showed me a picture of a bookish but pretty woman with blonde hair pulled tightly into a bun.

He'd boxed me in again. Even while attempting to be friendly, Randy had forced me into an uncomfortable situation: "If you have someone?" Now I had to have "someone."
"Oh sure, Randy. I can bring someone."
"Wonderful. I didn't know that you had a special someone."
"Yes, her name is Julia. Julia Robertson."
"Well then, Suzanne and I cannot wait to meet Ms. Robertson. I've never heard you talk about her. What does she do?"
"Um. She's self-employed, but has a bunch of clients. Very specialized work. It's a kind of physical therapy. She's a physical therapist."
"Noble work. I bet she's a good soul." Randy extended his hand.
"She's a regular Mother Teresa," I said, shaking it.
"I have to return to the center, but will see you Friday at four. I suggest Sun Lok Ki on Mott Street, just south of Canal. I look forward to meeting your Julia."
It was only a block to the subway, but my phone was out and I texted furiously the whole way.
"U there. Do u want to come to early dinner w/me and friends on Fri?"
The response came back immediately. "OK. Friday is good worknight. $200 and done by 9. ☺"
"No. Dinner is early- tween lunch and dinner. Linner @ 4, meet at 3. U and me. Done by 7. U can work full night."
"OK with linner, $100 and done by 7. ☺"
"Maybe you just come 2 linner w/ me. Just 4 fun. Not work?"
"OMG. U mean a date, Prof? ☹"
"Yes. Date. If u want to call it that."
"No. $100. But friends will think it a date. Done by 7. ☺"
My heart sank. I texted, "OK, meet me at the Starbucks on Canal @ 3:00." This would give us an hour to develop

a plausible boyfriend-girlfriend scenario that would withstand Randy's prying.

⁂

THE STARBUCKS on Canal Street sits in the middle of Chinatown. It may be the only Starbucks in the United States where the menu items are listed in Chinese characters, with the English translation underneath in tiny letters. Self-important young Asian women, dressed in the best threads Lord & Taylor offers, double park their Lexus SUVs outside without a second thought, bringing traffic to a halt. They get a Caramel Macchiato Grande before driving back to Queens or Jersey. Conventional wisdom is that, even in the middle of the day, lines are always long at the Chinatown Starbucks. I affirmed the conventional wisdom as I fell into a twenty-deep line at 3:05.

By now, I expected Julia to be late. I told her to meet me at three, hoping she'd show up at three fifteen. But it was not until 3:28 that Julia arrived. She was a head taller than most of the patrons and her curly auburn hair bounced on top of the sea of tightly pressed heads of black straight hair.

I waved to her. But it was obvious that she'd already seen me. She waved back and came toward me.

She reached me as I reached the counter. She kissed me lightly on the lips. "Sorry I'm late. You can order my usual, hon."

"What's your usual?"

"Oh, you're funny, Matt. Come on. After two and a half years together, you know my Starbucks faves better than me. Go ahead and order."

I understood. Julia was already in character, showing me how well she could play the part of my adoring girlfriend.

I ordered and we were given two steaming cups of strong coffee. With no seats inside, we moved onto the busy street. "Follow me. There're some benches over there." Julia took a cup from me. "So what's the backstory, Professor. You're James Dean and I'm Natalie Wood? You're Tobey Maguire and I'm Kirsten Dunst? You're Shia LaBeouf and I'm Megan Fox?"

"I'm Matt Hristahalios, a financially teetering academic, and you're Julia Robertson, a physical therapist."

"Julia Robertson? Oh, now that's original. I don't know shit about physical therapy, Professor. Couldn't I be something simple, like a nuclear physicist?"

Reaching an empty bench, I sat down. "Physical therapy, come on. It's easy. You work with people—old people, injured people—and you do little exercises with them to restore their strength and coordination."

"What kind of exercises? Something like this?" Julia stepped up on the bench and stepped across me with one leg. She lowered herself over me, her perfect little boobs brushing my face through a thin sweater, straddling me in ultratight jeans that left nothing to the imagination. Completely uninhibited, she started dry humping me on the bench, "One, two, three. One, two, three. I love these exercises, Professor. You'll be a new man in no time, baby." She kissed me hard on the lips; she had that funny metallic taste in her mouth again.

I was embarrassed, amused, and aroused all at the same time. "You're making me crazy, Julia."

She leaned in close and whispered. "I know, Professor. Your boner's big enough to split poor little me in half." Then she dismounted and sat next to me. She winked at the two young Chinese men pointing at us and clucking loudly in Cantonese.

"We have twenty minutes to finish the backstory. Here's what I'm thinking. You're a physical therapist, but we'll try to keep things as close to real as we can, so everything's easy to remember. You live in Alphabet City. We met through a common friend at the graduate school in midtown."

"Yep. But I am totally gaga for you, Professor. I can barely keep my hands off you, right?"

"You're gaga enough, but don't hump me in the restaurant."

"That'll be hard, Professor. Julia Robertson, physical therapist, gets wet from just sitting at the same table with a certain hunky underpaid junior professor."

"Well, she'll have to control herself. Here are our stories: We've only been on a few dates with each other. I don't know all that much about you. You don't know all that much about me. But we'll need to know the basics. Here's my bio: I'm from Morris, Illinois, a small town 80 miles from Chicago. My father was a GI for twenty years who saved up enough money to buy a small mechanic shop when he got out. He now restores old trucks mostly. My mom died five years ago. I have no brothers or sisters. I came to New York seven years ago to do grad work in sociology at NYU and got my PhD last December. Now, I'm on a postdoc, and you know something about my interest in prostitutes."

She nodded.

"Okay, your turn. Tell me your story."

"It can be anything you want it to be. You already made me a physical therapist."

"I understand, but besides swapping physical therapy for hooking, tell me the truth. It'll be easiest for you and me to remember."

"Just make up something, Professor. I'll remember it."

"Just tell me the truth, Julia. The guy we're meeting with is not really a friend. Randy Skiles is the other 2013 fellow at the center, and we barely pretend to like each other. He's like a super-intelligent frenemy from one of those reality TV shows. But the stakes are higher. He's out to degrade me and my work because, if he outshines me, it will enhance the perception that he's the exceptional scholar. I think he's using this linner as a chance to peek into my personal life, to see if he can find out anything about me that can be used against me later on. So give me your bio, a bio you know back to front. He's a bright guy on a mission—he'll find us out if we're not airtight. What's your bio?"

Julia flushed. "This is bullshit, Professor. I didn't come here to get grilled by some intellectual snot with a hard-on for bringing you down. I don't know shit about physical therapy; I don't know shit about you."

She stood up and started walking away. "You ain't Dr. Phil and I ain't gonna tell you about my past. I don't need this fuckin' linner with the frenemy."

I shot after her and took her arm. She wheeled around. For a second, I thought she was going to punch me. Her cheeks were red and eyes puffy. I felt awful for her. For all her confidence and streetwise glib, she now appeared fragile. We stared at each other for a second. I wanted to kiss her. I wanted to tell her that whatever was hard about her past, I would make it okay.

"Professor, the only way to do this is for you to give me a bio. Whatever you tell me, I will know it. Trust me. I'm good at pretending—it's what I do for a living."

⁕

Twenty minutes later, we entered Sun Lok Ki. Chinatown restaurants are the polar opposite of what people imagine to be the Manhattan dining experience. They are dirty and void of décor. People seated at the front tables inevitably are jostled by irritable patrons waiting for takeout; people seated at the back tables inevitably are jostled by underage kitchen hands carrying crates of provisions into the cooking area. The restaurants are too small to have any good tables in between. But even the most snobby Manhattanite loves Chinatown for its authenticity and working-class grit. Grad students further love it because it's the cheapest place on the island to get a good meal and nearly every subway line stops there.

Randy and Suzanne already were seated. They both were wearing turtlenecks and wire-rimmed glasses. Randy's fiancée shared his straight hair and L.L. Bean-model attractiveness. They easily could have been mistaken for brother and sister.

"Good to see you, Matthew, and wonderful to meet you, Julia. Matthew has told me so much about you." Randy extended his hand to me.

I shook his hand, "Yeah, tons, Randy." Julia smiled and shook Randy's hand also.

I extended my hand across the table, "Hello, Suzanne, I am Matt Hristahalios. This is Julia Robertson."

Randy held out a chair for Julia as she sat down. The menus were already at the table but Randy grabbed them up and stated, "This place has a Cantonese-only menu with some wonderful foods that are not available on the regular menu. My Cantonese isn't great, but with Suzanne's help I think we can manage to find some special dishes. Julia, do you think you can convince Matthew to let us order? We'll take you on a culinary tour of South China." Randy looked at me, "And Matthew, don't worry, we'll interrupt that tour to order General Tso's Chicken as well."

Julia gave me a cockeyed look, "A culinary tour of South China sounds fine, Randy."

A small Chinese-only menu was placed in front of them. For the next five minutes Randy and Suzanne argued in combinations of Chinese and English phrases about the best kind of noodle, whether or not to order tofu, and whether the fish in the front tank was sea bass. As best I could tell, Suzanne wanted the fish, but only if it was sea bass.

After ordering, the dishes started arriving quickly. Julia and I listened to Randy and Suzanne exchange facts about Chinese art and literature. I found myself wondering if they were always this pretentious, or if they too were playacting.

Finally, Randy looked up, "So, Julia, do you have a favorite book about China?"

"Well, I don't know too many, but," she started laughing. "I really liked *Yellow River* by I.P. Daily."

On that old grade school standby, I spit out a mouthful of General Tso's Chicken. It left a string of circular gravy stains on the bleached-white tablecloth before finally stopping halfway across the table.

I pointed to the tablecloth. "Julia reminds me of my favorite Chinese novel, *Brown Spots* by Hu Flung Poo." Julia and I started laughing like Bart Simpson and Milhouse after a well-executed crank call to Moe's Tavern.

Things took off from there. The book titles just kept coming:

Julia: "Matt, did you read *The Bearded Chinaman* by Harry Chin?"

Me: "Sure, I liked that one better than *Boring Stories* by Ime Yaw Ning."

Julia: "Here's one: *Sex with an Old Chinese Man* by Rink Li Dong."

We moved off China and kept riffing on punny book titles: *The Star Wars Sedan Chair* by Carrie Walker; *Low-Calorie Cooking Made Easy* by M.T. Potts; *Condom in My Wallet* by Justin Case; *Embracing Suicide* by Watts DePointe.

Even Suzanne got into the act, calling out with great self-satisfaction. "Oh, I know one. How about *Too Big to Fail* by Warren T. Banks?" She clapped and giggled at her cleverness. Julia and I laughed with her. Randy made eye contact with Suzanne and scowled. She suppressed herself.

But Randy's sour face couldn't keep us from starting up again: *Back from the Dead* by Frank N. Stine; *Frankenstein's*

Uncultured Sister by Phyllis Stine; *Twisted Sister Goes to Russia* by Ivana Rock; *Russia's Dumbest Man* by Yuri Tarded.

Finally, I called out what I was sure was the best one of the night: "Julia, Suzanne. I got one that you cannot top. *Cat in My Underpants* by Claude Ball. Game, set and match." I waved my hands to an imaginary adoring crowd.

Randy sat stone-faced through it all, which made every jokey book title that much funnier. Julia made a pouty face at him. Then she stood up and slithered across the table suggestively toward Randy pulling up six inches from him. She leaned forward so her cleavage was in his face. "Randy, babe, you wanna know my favorite book of all time? It's *Stop Staring at My Tits, You Pretentious Twit* by Eileen Dover."

That brought down the house. Tears streamed down my face. Suzanne busted open, too. Randy blushed and nervously sipped tea. Everyone in the restaurant was staring at us.

Julia took a napkin and wiped the tears from her eyes, and then she wiped the tears from my face. She took fifty dollars from her purse and plunked it down on the table. "Suzanne, I've really enjoyed laughing with you. You too, Randy, hope you didn't mind me kidding around."

She leaned into my ear. "Let's go to my place, Professor. I'm going to fuck your brains out." We left a still-giggling Suzanne and a gape-jawed Randall Skiles.

IT WAS a short walk to Julia's apartment, four blocks north of Chinatown. She unlocked the small, non-descript door between a grocery and a hair salon and led me up a narrow staircase. We passed one door, and she unlocked a second.

We entered a small, tenement-style apartment. She left me standing in a narrow front living room and disappeared into a bathroom. I walked into a small galley

Conversation with Dad: October 7, 2012

I was still feeling incredibly good a couple of days later when Dad called for his regular Sunday morning check in.

"Yelloooow," I purred into the phone.

"How you doin', Matt. You sound happy."

"I am and I've already signed your petition: the one about letting vets go to Vietnam to recover the lost possessions of dead servicemen. I can get behind that one."

"Great. I've already got 150 signatures on it. But that's not why you're so happy."

"It's been a good few days."

"Is that because of this girlfriend of yours?"

"Mostly."

Dad was silent.

"Dad, were you ever really in love with Mom?"

"Oh, hell yes. I know you don't remember your mom and dad as the perfect couple. We certainly had some terrible fights toward the end. But you can't know how happy she made me as a young man, how much I used to think about her. It was so simple when we first started dating. Everything just seemed right when I was around her. That's all I needed for many years."

"I am glad to hear you say that, Dad. I think I feel that way about Julia."

"That's pretty serious. You've never had serious feelings for a girl. Go slow. You're younger than your years on this one."

"I know Mom had bad habits that she never fully kicked, habits that ultimately killed her. Julia has some bad habits, too."

"Matty, I need to ask you straight up. Is Julia a hooker?"

"No, Dad. She isn't. I have to go."

CHAPTER 7

Through Hook or Crook

The euphoria from besting Randy and having wonderful, nontransactional sex with Julia passed after a few more days. I knew that Julia would resent me behaving like a possessive boyfriend, so I gave her space. But I finally texted her, and I kept it simple. "Hey, call me or stop by." I waited for a reply that never came.

Over the next few days, I tried to put Julia out of my head and get moving on my research. I wasted a whole afternoon at the graduate school library, unable to focus on the microfilmed dissertation about Los Angeles prostitutes that had just arrived. I couldn't stop thinking about Julia—the beautiful woman who gave me a prime earning night—free of charge. In three and a half hours at the library, I read twenty pages, and didn't remember a word of the dissertation.

The next day, I attempted to map out a research budget for my interviews. Because I had been dipping into the $1,500 budget from the center to fund activities with Julia and her friends, I was already down to $900. Assuming I needed to get thirty valid interviews—the minimum sample size preferred by researchers seeking statistical validity—I had a mere thirty dollars to spend on each interview and follow-up intervention. My experience to date suggested that I would need about fifty dollars for an hour with a prostitute. So I was in trouble. But if I conducted my interviews in the middle of the day when their time was less valuable, I might still be able to convince enough hookers to talk to me. But I couldn't pinch from the research kitty again and still have any hope of completing my work.

The grim budget news was only a short distraction from thinking about Julia. I tried playing it cool. I knew the worst thing I could do was act like a smitten teen with a crush on the popular girl. One text to Julia was enough.

Then, on Wednesday, I caved. I texted: "UT? Cum 4 dinner soon. Miss U."

No response. That second text broke the dam. I texted her a half-dozen more times over the next two days. No response.

On Thursday, I received an e-mail from the graduate school's IRB. They had considered my research plan, and decided it could not be approved as submitted. In addition to technical questions about the protocol, they needed me to add a bunch of disclaimer language to my interview script and project materials. I also had to develop a formal list of sites and providers for the proposed interventions. I wouldn't be allowed to begin my field research until the materials were resubmitted, rereviewed, and approved.

I was too wrapped around thinking about Julia to respond. Dr. Beckwith called me on Friday and I let his call ring to voicemail. Playing the message later, I heard him ask diplomatically if I wanted some assistance responding to the IRB. I ignored his message.

Everywhere I went, the bodega, the local pizzeria, the coffee shop, I saw Julia. On every sidewalk, every woman with a decent ass became Julia. On Saturday, although I promised myself a thousand times I wouldn't do it, I walked across the Brooklyn Bridge into Manhattan. I walked past Julia's Holiday Inn apartment near Chinatown: The scene of that wonderful night a week earlier. I loitered outside, imagining seeing Julia coming out of the apartment and imagining her thrilled reaction to seeing me. I walked into

Alphabet City past the apartment building where I had played poker with her; then I walked past the Buzz Kill where we first met. I imagined bumping into her on the crowded street. I imagined her kissing me a friendly hello and asking me to stay with her for the afternoon.

I saw Julia everywhere I went. It was the beginning of what a psychiatrist might label an unhealthy obsession. After four hours of wandering around, I willed myself back to Brooklyn.

I went back to my apartment and slipped *Pretty Woman* into the DVD player. The real Julia Roberts never disappoints. At nine on Saturday night—when normal people across America are enjoying the best night of the week with friends—I beat off for the hundredth time to the real Julia Roberts in that short skirt, and then fell asleep.

Six hours later, I was jolted awake by a pounding at my door.

"Who's that?"

"Professor, open the door."

I turned on the lights and unbolted the door. Julia entered.

Although my eyes were still adjusting to the light, I could tell there was something wrong with her. Her eyes were bloodshot, she was shivering.

"Thought it was going to take you an hour to open the door, babe." She pushed past me and went into the bathroom, then came out and flopped on my bed.

"I like your bed. Mind if I crash here tonight? I don't feel great."

I was a little excited, but very uneasy. Something was wrong. I could hardly speak. "Um, that's fine."

She took off her skirt, blouse, and bra. Then she grabbed a T-shirt of mine off the floor and put it on. Within five minutes of entering the apartment she was in my bed under the blanket. I was still standing near the door.

I sat near the bed and watched her. I looked closely at her face: Without makeup and her wiseass banter to conceal the fact, she looked older—pushing forty. I could see veins in her face and little crow's feet at the corners of her eyes. She was still attractive, but also flawed and tired. She fell into a strange kind of sleep, shivering under my heavy blanket. Her breathing was shallow and fast. She wasn't speaking but her lips kept moving. I suppose a gentleman would have slept on the couch that night, but she looked so sad and helpless. She needed me.

I got into my bed and spooned her. I think my presence quieted her. She didn't stop shivering, but her breathing became more regular; her sleep deepened.

Sometime that night we had sex. I don't exactly know how it started; I was groggy. But I remember being on top of her and pushing myself hard into her. She groaned, but it wasn't at all like the groans of pleasure from a week earlier. It was a sad groan. As I exploded into her, she slurred. "Pull out, Professor." But it was too late.

I spooned her again. She whimpered as she fell back into a shallow sleep; her tears dripped on my forearm underneath her head. I pulled her close, gently kissed the damp back of her neck, and nodded off.

I AWOKE around dawn to a scurrying sound. The apartment was only dark shadows but I could still see a little. I saw Julia with a little flashlight at the mantle. She was in my research kitty, taking my money.

I bolted upright and came across to her. I became aware of my nakedness when she dug her nails into my upper arm. "I'm taking $200 for last night's rape, Professor. And if you ever put your thing in me again without a raincoat on it, I will have it cut off. No shit, Professor—I know people who will do it to you and laugh about it." Her voice lowered and she growled at me. "You can fuck me, Professor, but don't ever fuck with me."

I tried to reach out and pull her close, but her nails slashed across my chest. I wanted to hold her and apologize. I wanted to have a warm moment and explain that I was asleep. I wasn't even sure if I had initiated the sex.

My hand brushed gently across her face. She bit savagely into my thumb, hard enough to break skin, hard enough for me to yelp as her teeth crashed into knuckle bone.

I backed off, holding my thumb, dazed and grief stricken. And then she was gone without another word.

It took an hour for the nurse practitioner in the emergency room to clean my wound and close it with six stitches. Over the next few days, I winced in pain every time I attempted to lift a fork or write my name. Since I had to sign a ton of forms for the IRB on the resubmitted materials, there was plenty of wincing.

Dad called me twice that Sunday. I let him ring to voicemail both times. It wasn't until the following Sunday that I was ready to talk to him.

Conversation with Dad: October 21, 2012

It was eight thirty A.M. when Dad called, two hours earlier than usual. But I was awake, not having slept more than five hours any night since the fight with Julia.

"How ya doin', Matty. You're a hard guy to reach. That girlfriend runnin' you all over town?"

"Not exactly, Dad."

"Well, what's going on? You know I like to check in with you on Sunday mornings. I have three Sunday rituals: the Bears, picking a new petition, and calling you."

"Maybe you should try going back to church Dad. I'm sure Father Dimitri would love to see you again."

"I'm sure he'd love to see you, too, Matt. I'm not the atheist. My soul isn't doomed."

"I don't have a soul, Dad. Neither do you. Neither does Father Dimitri. But if I'm wrong, then my soul owes your soul a beer in heaven and you can gloat for eternity. Is that okay?"

"It's not okay, because when you talk like this, you make it harder for your soul to get into heaven. I guess I'm not all that helpful to you on Earth, much less in the hereafter. It makes me sad, Matty, knowing that you don't believe. You sound sad, too."

"I am sad, but not because of my doomed soul. It's because I'm under a lot of pressure. My research is behind schedule and I'm underfunded. I have to use my living allowance to cover my research. And my living allowance barely covers rent and groceries. It's not right."

"Can't you get some more money from your center?"

"I don't think so, Dad. They'll want receipts for everything. I don't have receipts. As you might guess, prostitutes aren't real big on receipts." I looked down at the stitches on my thumb, and thought about the hundred dollar emergency room co-pay that I paid out of the research kitty. Between this and the $200 Julia took from it, I had only

$600 left. It would never be enough for thirty interviews, much less any post-interview interventions.

"Rent is due at the end of the month. I'm in danger of not making a rent payment for the first time in my life."

The other side of the phone was silent.

"Are you there, Dad?"

He sighed. "Being a good parent sometimes means letting your child suffer a little. I love you, Sonny Boy, but you have to live within your means. Cut back on expenses with this girlfriend; get a night job. Maybe you should do both." There was another pause on the phone. "But maybe I can help you a little. Let me think about this. When we talk next week, I'll have an answer."

"Thanks, Dad, I'll call you next Sunday. And I will take a look at your latest petition. I promise."

"I know you will, Matty. You need the money."

CHAPTER 8

Depraving the Hooker

October 21 was the day that my negative cash flow problem matured into financial crisis. My Amex card came due: $1,700 that I didn't have. This was mostly due to the extra charges from my weekend with Will and Tim, and my adventures with Julia and her friends. I was already carrying $1,100 in debt on my Visa.

I had no choice. I cashed my $2,000 monthly stipend check at one of those awful 24-7 payday lenders. I used most of the money to pay off my Amex, and used the remaining $300 to replenish my diminished bank account, which now doubled to $600. There was no way I was going to make it through the month—I'd spend half that on General Tso alone. I wouldn't even make rent in ten days.

While my heart was still stuck on Julia, my brain was moving toward despising her. My financial situation had always been precarious, but Julia had pushed me off the fiscal cliff. On top of that, she groundlessly accused me of rape and sent me to the hospital with a deep incision on my thumb.

The time had come to see her again. Not as a patsy, not as a john, but as a lover who had taken enough abuse. I would find her, tell her off, and take back my money—by force if necessary.

I WALKED the Brooklyn Bridge back into Manhattan and headed for Julia's apartment. I propped myself up in a doorway across the street and steeled myself for a long wait. That turned out to be a bad plan. I waited five hours in an autumn drizzle. She never appeared. Finally, I went home.

The next day I went to her apartment again. I waited six hours. I went home again.

I resolved to try one more time. In a light but cold rain, I propped myself up inside the doorway across the street from her apartment and waited. Only thirty minutes later, I saw her. She was walking up the street with a short, old guy in an overcoat and a dark suit—a john, I was sure.

I watched Julia unlock the door and sprinted across the street as they entered. My foot wedged inside the doorjamb before the door shut. I slinked inside and tiptoed up the stairs behind them.

The older guy was just closing the apartment door as I came onto the landing and pushed my shoulder through the door.

There was terror in his eyes. He picked up an umbrella and thrust it toward me as if it were a sword.

I pushed its tip out of my way. "Who are you, the Penguin?" My hands balled into fists.

Julia put herself in between us. "Professor, this is Richard. Richard, this is the professor."

"Richard? Oh, Richard Gere and Julia Roberts, of course. You're Richard Gere. But you're five foot five and you defend your woman with an umbrella. What kind of lame fantasy is this? Get the fuck out of here, Richard Gere. This movie is over."

"Well, what's your fantasy, Mr. Professor. Is Julia your hot little coed? Like that's not sick." Again, he waved the umbrella menacingly at me.

I looked to Julia, "Tell this dickhead that I really am a professor and then get rid of him."

Julia pulled the umbrella out of Richard Gere's hands. "Richard, babe, the professor's all riled up. I'm sorry, but

I'm going to have to deal with this Mad Professor alone for a little while." She kissed her hand and put it on his cheek. "Let's pick this up again next week. I promise to make it up to you." She hugged him and turned him toward the door.

"Are you going to be okay with this nut?" he asked.

"The professor is an asshole, but I don't think he's dangerous." She glared at me. "At least not while I'm awake." Then she gently nudged Richard out of the apartment and closed the door.

She wheeled around, "Hey, asshole! That man pays my rent. And whatever you think of his fantasy, he's always been kind to me." She looked at me accusingly, "Where do you get off breaking into my apartment, Professor? What kind of psycho stalker are you?"

"Who's the psycho? You showed up at my place in the middle of the night all spaced out on something. We fell asleep and had sex during the night. I don't even think I started it. Then you steal my money, accuse me of rape, and assault me. If there's only one psycho in this room, it's not me. Give me my money and I am out of your life. Ignore me, and you've got a crazy john on your hands."

She was going to attack me again. I tensed up as she moved toward me; my hands balled back into fists.

But she didn't attack me. Instead, she leaned in close and kissed me underneath the ear. "You got balls after all, Professor. Good for you." She whispered, "I'm not going to talk about money anymore. But I am going to get you high and then fuck you like there's no tomorrow."

"No . . ." I started to say. But her hands were up my shirt and her lips were on mine. The adrenaline flowed out of my fists and into my penis.

Soon she was sucking me off on the couch. Our clothes were mostly off. Then she pulled away and pulled a little square mirror from her purse. As she did this, I ran my tongue up and down her backbone and bit at her perfect butt. She yelped a little, but could not be distracted. Before I even noticed, there were four neat lines on the mirror. She sniffed up one and handed me the rolled-up dollar bill.

I had smoked pot a half-dozen times in my life but never liked it much. A few times at NYU I had the chance to try other drugs but each time turned them down. But now here was the most beautiful woman in the world, the woman who had taken my heart, my virginity, and my money, offering me cocaine as a peace offering. I briefly considered saying no. Then I grabbed up the dollar bill and sniffed the line in a giant snort.

My nose hairs singed and throttled in pain. I nearly gagged on the metallic taste that choked me at the back of my mouth and throat. It must have shown on my face. Julia laughed. "There's nothing cuter than a coke virgin." She did another line and slid me the mirror and dollar bill. I snorted again. This one burned too, but less intensely.

She went to her iPod docking station and selected a special song. "Professor, have you ever heard *'Eighty-Eight Lines about Forty-Four Women.'* I've been grinding to this song since I was fifteen." An electronic drum and thumping bass started playing. A man started speak-singing about the dozens of wild women he'd screwed.

Then she was all over me: a mass of arms grabbing at me, a dozen lips kissing my chest and licking my balls, eight or twelve tits rubbing all over me. It was amazing. Suddenly, she pulled away to sing a few lines from the crazy song:

> Xylla was an archetype, the voodoo queen the
>   queen of rap.
> Joan thought men were second best at masturbating
>   in the bath.
> Sherri was a feminist, she really had that gift of gab.
> Kathleen's point of view was this: take whatever
>   you can grab.

Then she was on me again, grabbing my dick and rubbing it hard. I was aggressive with her, too, kissing the insides of her thighs, sometimes biting them—once perhaps too hard, judging by the squeal it induced. She started singing again.

> Well Rhonda had a house in Venice, lived on brown rice and cocaine.
> Patty had a house in Houston, shot cough syrup in her veins.
> Linda thought her life was empty, filled it up with alcohol.
> Katherine was much too pretty, she didn't do that shit at all.

I picked her up and carried her across the little apartment into the kitchen and put her on the counter, I went into her, and then pulled out. She whispered, "Let's go now." I whispered back, "I'll fuck you when I'm ready."

I carried her into her bedroom, biting at her on each step. She kept singing her song:

> Bobbie joined a new-wave band, and changed her name to Bobbie-sox.
> Eloise who played guitar, sang songs about whales and cops.
> Terri didn't give a shit, just a nihilist.
> Ronnie was much more my style, she wrote songs just like this.

> Jezebel went forty days drinking nothing but Perrier.
> Dinah drove her Chevrolet into the San Francisco bay.
> Judy came from O-hi-o, she's a Scientologist.
> Amiranta, here's a kiss, I chose you to end this list.

We tumbled onto the bed. She grabbed my rock-hard erection and put it inside her. We had sick, crazy, sweaty cocaine sex. I don't know really how long I was hard, but it was long enough to get her off twice before I came into her. And then, after a twenty-minute break, we did it again. This time I put her up on the kitchen counter and I rammed myself into her until it hurt.

Sweaty and exhausted I went into the bathroom to wash my face and penis. Julia returned to her bed. She was lying on her back with her legs open, gently fanning her vag. I joined her on the bed and we fell quickly asleep.

Four hours later, I woke up. The apartment smelled of sweat and sex. The cocaine had worn off and my mouth tasted awful. But I felt good. Perhaps I shouldn't admit this, but I was proud: Proud that I stood up to her john, however hapless he was; proud that I stood up to Julia; proud that I had brought Julia to orgasm; proud that Julia, even though she could never admit it, was behaving like she had feelings for me.

I started dressing. Julia rolled over, "Professor, are you leaving?"

"Yeah, Julia, time for me to go home. Can I see you again?"

"Sure, babe."

"Will I have to pay?"

"Of course, babe. I like you but I'm a working girl. Business is business, even for preferred clients. Just give me $200 for last night, babe. The coke was my gift to you. I feel bad about biting you."

After all the shit I'd endured; after all the debt, the bite, and the robbery; after real intimacy, I was still only a john. My anger rose.

"Two hundred dollars? You gotta be kidding me. You robbed me two weeks ago, Julia." I put on my sweater and headed for the exit.

She bolted upright, still naked. "Don't turn your back on me, you tiny-dicked egghead." In just a second she'd gone from bed-headed and groggy to wild-eyed and pissed off. "Don't you dare walk out on me with an unsettled bill, Professor."

I ignored her and opened the apartment door.

A wine bottle whizzed past my head and shattered against the door. Glass shards and red wine splashed all over me. My clothes were stained with purple splotches from the chest down.

I slammed the door behind me and got the hell out of there. Curses and crying filled the stairwell as I hustled away from the crazy woman inside the apartment.

My heartbeat didn't return to normal until I reached Brooklyn.

Conversation with Dad: October 28, 2012

I called Dad at nine on Sunday morning.
"Hello."
"Hi, Dad. How you doin'?"
"Fine, Matty. Why'd you call?"
"I called because we always speak on Sunday mornings. Remember, I'm your surrogate church. You've said that yourself."
"Is that right?" Dad sounded distant.
"Is something wrong, Dad?"
"Well, let me ask you a question. We speak most Sundays, but, before today, when was the last time you called me?"
"Not sure, maybe a month ago?"
"It was August, Matty. August 9. This is the first time you've called me in almost three months."
"Yeah, maybe. I guess it's been a while. What's your point, Dad?"
"My point is that this is the first time you've called me in something like eleven weeks. And half the times I've called you, you've given me the bum's rush and shoved me off the phone after a few minutes. But now you call me the week after you tell me you need money. It doesn't leave your old man feeling a lot of warm and fuzzies."
"You got me wrong. Sure I need money, but that's not what motivated this call." I paused, I didn't want to say it, but Dad's hurt feelings had boxed me in. "I was motivated to call you Dad because, well, because of, this may sound funny, but because of Mom."
"Mom?"
"Yeah, Dad, it's about Mom and Julia, my girlfriend. I think they're alike. Mom was an amazing person, but self-destructive. Julia is wired just like Mom—really smart, high energy, and wild. But she's dangerous. I remember Mom getting drunk and swearing up a storm. I remember

when she hit you. I remember you carrying her away so I wouldn't see her crazy moments." I teared up. "Dad, Julia bit me a few weeks ago. I needed six stitches; yesterday she threw a wine bottle at me. I'd probably be in the hospital today if that bottle hit me. I can't see her anymore. But Dad, I might love her. It's crazy, I know. But I think I love her."

"Oh shit, Matty. Don't fall in love with someone like that. Find a nice, boring girl. This Julia sounds worse than your mother. I had some wonderful times with your Mom, but it wasn't worth it. There were times when I had to restrain her; other times I had to take you over to the Okerson's so you wouldn't see her after she messed herself up. She messed up her own body a bunch of times—once stabbed herself in the arm. It was so ugly. You don't want that. Don't repeat your old man's mistakes."

"Dad, this is the first time you've ever really leveled with me about Mom. You've always whitewashed her crazy moments."

"It's the first time I've had to level with you. A father doesn't want to talk bad to his son about his mother. It's not right. But now, because of what you've told me, I have to. My mother was always a bit crazy, not as bad as your mother, but capable of huge mood swings. Then I married your mother—God rest her soul. Looking back, she probably should have spent the second half of her life in a psych ward. You've heard those old songs about sons being destined to marry someone just like their mothers. I don't want that for you."

"It's more than an old song, Dad. Respected shrinks like John Money at Harvard said that images of our parents make imprints in our minds as children. These images become the template for the people we seek out as companions later in life. The templates are not unbreakable, but they do create strong tendencies."

"Well, break the tendency," Dad interrupted. "You have your whole life ahead of you. You don't need to tie yourself to someone who might hurt you, or might hurt herself and leave you to clean up the mess. I'm buying you a plane ticket to come home. Take my advice and leave New York for a few months. Put some space between you and her. If you need money, I have some for you. It's waiting for you here in Morris. If this Julia's what you tell me she is, she's not going to stay away from you. And if she's got half the gifts of your mother, you won't be able to turn her away."

"I told you I'm going cold turkey on Julia. You're going to need to trust me, Dad. Let's keep the dates flexible, but I'll try to come home over Christmas break."

I hung up the phone, and was overcome by sadness. For the next hour, I sobbed.

CHAPTER 9

The Odds are Good, but the Goods are Odd

Purging Julia from my life facilitated my most productive week since coming to the center. I finished up all the disclaimers and administrative bullshit needed by the IRB, and received official permission to begin my field research. With Rachel Rubenstein's help, I was introduced to a couple of Brooklyn-based social workers who worked out of battered-women's shelters. They introduced me to several ex-hookers in their care: They were the skanky crack-ho types who grossed me out. Still, it was now time to get serious about my research and I needed to get over my hang-ups. So in exchange for providing the shelters with a fifty-dollar contribution, I received invitations to interview these women.

I began writing up my hooker movie and book notes into an annotated bibliography—a requirement for the end of the semester. I listed 375 sources by topic and wrote the first hundred annotations. Then I e-mailed the draft to Randy Skiles and requested his peer review (cc-ing Beckwith). The draft bibliography was already really good and there'd be no chance Randy's peer review would improve it. I knew that. So this was the perfect time to solicit a peer review from my pompous frenemy. Randy had no choice but to write, two days later, that he was impressed by my "obvious command of the pertinent scholarly research and popular content."

Money was still a huge problem, but instead of General Tso and pizza twice a day, I started making myself cheap, healthy meals like bean chili and spinach-and-feta omelets. I also started walking the dogs of the artsy couple that lived on the ground level of my row house. They have two huge but sweet Great Danes; I was paid thirty dollars a day for an hour spent with the drooling beasts. I did some budgeting and figured that I could live frugally on my stipend, and use the additional funds to start paying down my debts without help from Dad. My landlord, a heavy Lithuanian named Davydos, was surprisingly easygoing about me being late on the rent. Because I'd been a reliable tenant for seven years, he had no concerns with me falling behind this once. We worked out a schedule where I'd make $150 supplemental payments (in addition to regular rent) twice a month, for four months to make it up. So I had to live like a starving grad student again. But I'd lived this way for the last seven years before the fellowship and I would do so again.

As for Julia, Dad was right. She tried to reengage me. Twice she texted me: The first time, she was apologetic: "Hey. Sorry. Can we talk?" The second time, her text was either humorous or vaguely menacing: "Don't ignore me, Prof. I know where you live." But I was making good on my pledge to go cold turkey on her. I ignored her—that is until she showed up.

THAT THURSDAY night, as always, I exited the subway on Atlantic Avenue, walked three blocks, and turned the block for my apartment. There she was. We made eye contact. She gave me a friendly little wave. I crossed the street and walked right past her.

"Hey Dickhead," she shouted. "I'm pregnant. And this piece of shit inside of me is yours. Everyone else I've been with in the last two months had the brains to wear a raincoat."

A shiver of horror overtook my body. I felt nauseous. Knees wobbling, I crossed the street to her. "My God, Julia. Are you really pregnant?"

"Nah. I'm on the pill. I knew you weren't carrying anything bad, so I let you cum inside me as a perk. No fuss for you and no risk to me." She giggled, "Geez, Professor. You look so friggin' scared. Sorry baby. I just needed to say something that would shock you. So you'd talk to me again." She kissed me on the cheek. "I miss you, Professor."

Four times over the next four minutes, I showed resolve: "I can't see you, Julia." "You're bad for me." "We're oil and water." "I'm just a simple Midwest guy; you're messing up my mind." Each time, she smiled, "But I miss you, Professor."

Finally, she played her trump card. "Professor, I remember your research. You're supposed to be meeting sex-working girls like me and determining if we can be saved. So, here you go, Professor: Save me. I want to be good. Make me Doris Day. It's so cute." That was it. She had me.

"Jesus, Julia, you've complicated my simple life."

"Maybe so, but I'm better company than hooker movies and wet sheets. I got some good times in my purse, you get some wine. Let's have a little party at your place, Professor. Just the two of us, the best kind of party."

I resisted the urge to kiss her. "No. Our relationship is now strictly research. It's cold. I will buy you a plate of stew from the Polish place on Atlantic, and that's only for research purposes. We'll discuss if you can, indeed, be saved. But that's it. You're just a prostitute in my study, okay?" I grinned, I couldn't stop myself.

"Whatever you say, Professor. I am just hooker Number 37B in your study." As we walked toward the restaurant, she coiled herself under my arm and snuggled into me. I didn't move her away.

WITHIN A mile radius of my apartment, there are at least a hundred restaurants. Of these, probably two-thirds feature an international cuisine of one kind or another: Italian, Greek, Portuguese, German, Indian, Mideastern, Ethiopian, Mexican, Caribbean, Chinese, Vietnamese, and Thai. And of these restaurants, probably two-thirds are now owned by Koreans. Usually, the Koreans go through the formality of maintaining a token employee from the pertinent nationality and station the token employee at the front of the restaurant to lend a smidge of authenticity. Smiling Alojzy at the Little Warsaw Grill on Atlantic Avenue is a case in point: He smiles because he gets paid to smile. He also distributes menus to people as they arrive, but, as best I can tell, he doesn't do anything else. He insinuates with his presence that there is an old Polish matron in the kitchen. In reality, it's a young chain-smoking Korean guy with ugly tattoos across his body. A man named Kim sears the perogies and onions, stuffs the cabbage, boils the kielbasa, and fries the latkes. Koreans will soon own every restaurant in Brooklyn. I say this without animus: They learn the craft and hold down prices. I love Koreans.

"I haven't had Polish food since I was a little girl, Professor. This is a nice idea," Julia said as Alojzy, still smiling, handed us two menus and pointed us to a table in the half-filled little restaurant.

"Did you grow up in a Polish neighborhood, Julia?" I asked as we settled at the table. "If you're going to be subject Number 37B in my study, you have to tell me about your past and why you fell into prostitution."

A look of discomfort came over her face, as if I had caught her in a lie. "You know, Professor, I meant to say that I just like Polish food—real comfort food—and it's been a long time. What's your favorite, babe?"

"My favorite food is whatever you liked so much as a child, Julia. Tell me about your favorite Polish dish as a little girl. I'm sorry, but there's really no reason to continue together if you won't do this."

She was trapped; she finally had to tell me about her past. I tipped back in my chair happy to have captured her. Finally, she would come clean about her past, or I'd be rid of her once and for all. Either way, I'd win.

Julia looked around a little and bit a fingernail. "You know, Professor, I'm not real comfortable talking about my childhood. I had some Polish food as a girl and liked it. That's good enough. A hooker's childhood isn't part of your research. It's not, as you eggheads say, 'in scope.'"

"Well, Julia, I'm glad you've become such an expert on qualitative research methods, but actually, you're quite wrong. My final approved interview protocol includes asking the prostitute about her childhood." Sure, I was stretching the truth, but after all she'd put me through, I wasn't going to let her off easy.

"You see, Julia, I'm trying to establish if a particularly significant childhood incident correlates with prostitution later in life. So, if you don't want to tell me about your childhood, I can't include you in the study and perhaps we should go our separate ways. I hope you understand."

She gnawed at a second nail. "Well, Professor, this is a problem for us. I don't talk to people about my past. It's just a thing of mine, okay. Ask me something else, and I'll tell you whatever you'd like."

"I'm sorry if this is uncomfortable for you, but I need you to answer my question. Otherwise, we're at an impasse." I tipped back in my seat. Finally, I was in control—it was very satisfying.

She glanced around the restaurant. Then she leaned in toward me and waited for me to join her over the little table. I let her wait several seconds before finally leaning in.

Nearly whispering, she said, "All right, Professor. Here's what I can do for you. I will tell you about pieces of my childhood—other parts are behind a secret wall and nobody's ever been allowed there. And I will tell you how I came to New York and started hooking. That's more than anyone knows. Is that good enough for you?"

I tipped back in my chair again, elated at her proposal, but wanting to appear disappointed. I'd never furrowed my brow before (not even sure how to do it), but I attempted to furrow my brow anyway.

Finally, I leaned forward again. "Okay, Julia. This may be less than my protocol requires, but I'll make an exception for you. Give me enough about your childhood and how it might have led you into hooking and I won't pry beyond that. That's because you're a preferred client and *you* look so cute and clueless."

Over the next hour, Julia and I had our first real conversation. At times she was coldly honest, almost to the point of journalistic, about her past; at other times, she was evasive and emotional. I had to dig hard for the information she wouldn't initially offer. But for all her protestations, I think she was happy to finally open up to someone.

Julia was born eight years before me, in the dying mill town of Washington, Pennsylvania, outside of Pittsburgh. She spent her early childhood with her single mother who tried hard to raise her right, but worked two jobs and was never home. Julia never knew her father. She spent a lot of time under the care of a strict but slow-witted uncle who was old enough to be her grandfather. She learned to get what she wanted by tricking and manipulating him. At age thirteen, Julia's mother became sick with cancer and died a year later. Julia was sent to live with a crazy aunt in Wilkinsburg—another working class town near Pittsburgh. The crazy aunt had a crazier boyfriend who sexually abused Julia. Julia acted out in school, getting into a string of fights with both girls and boys. At fourteen, she became involved with a boy—he was nineteen. After their first fight, she doused his car with gasoline and set it on fire.

Social workers got involved. Julia was enrolled in psychiatric counseling, put on antidepressant drugs, and sent into foster care—which, as she described it, was a succession of nightmares. Twice, she attempted to run away. The first time was with a boyfriend on a motor scooter—they made it six miles before getting picked up by the police. The second time, she hitched halfway to Orlando before police picked her up and returned her to Pittsburgh. She ended up in a third foster home with five other kids, including a boy who raped her and threatened to kill her if she told anyone.

So she ran away again. This time she hitched to Seattle. The man who took her most of the way was a religious trucker; he was the first to notice her resemblance to the actress, Julia Roberts. He told her all about Alaska. He described it as the best place on earth for a pretty young girl to start fresh. In exchange for blow jobs every few hundred miles, he put some cash in her pocket, and bought her a package of L'Oréal auburn hair dye. On reaching Seattle, he bought her a one-way ticket to Alaska. Julia arrived there two weeks shy of eighteen, hoping to find a decent man with a steady job. All she had with her was a backpack stuffed with a change of clothes, sixty dollars, and a great ass. She didn't know a single person in the state.

Julia went straight to a bar near the airport and milled around, letting men buy her drinks and probing for a homeowner who wasn't an axe murderer. She ended up with a heavyset guy twice her age (she called him Ralph, but I think she was using the name metaphorically). Ralph owned a rundown cottage outside the city. She slept with him in exchange for room and board.

He performed odd jobs, and was gone for days at a time. She eventually came to know the neighbors and picked up a part-time job at the town's child-care center.

It wasn't the greatest life, but she liked working with the kids. At last, she was safe and warm. After a few years, she started thinking about marriage and kids of her own. Ralph wasn't attractive, but he treated her well and she came to love him.

Walking home from work one day, she saw a big woman in an old pickup parked in front of the cottage. The woman glared at her. Sensing trouble, Julia hustled past the truck toward the house. The woman came out of the truck and attacked Julia, beating her with a metal flashlight. Julia was left lying in the front yard with a dozen welts, a dislocated jaw, and a fractured wrist. The woman was Ralph's wife.

Julia ended up in the hospital and, upon release, had nowhere to go but to a homeless shelter in Anchorage. There, she met a man who introduced her to another man who ran an escort service. That man advanced Julia $200 to buy some "professional clothes" and drove her out to a large house near the fishing docks. The house included six other escorts. Men would come to the house and pick up the girl they wanted to date that night. The escort service charged $200 for a night with the women, more on weekends. The women were paid a standard fee of fifty dollars for a night out, plus any additional money they negotiated privately for sex. Julia came to know Alaska's sailors and fishermen as sad men with defective personalities: They were superstitious, ignorant, violent, irrational, and almost always alcoholic. Julia knew Alaska was filled with single men, but concluded there wasn't a decent man in the state. She came to believe the line frequently uttered by Alaskan women, "The odds are good, but the goods are odd."

Julia was the youngest of the escorts. Maybe because she was so young and pretty, men asked for Julia again and again. But Julia wouldn't do anything sexual with them. The other women hated her and started stealing her money. She resolved to leave the semibrothel after one of her dates attempted to rape her. He pinned her down on a motel bed. She swung wildly with a lamp, broke his arm, and ran. He couldn't hold her down.

She wanted to go to New York, which she had visited as a little girl. To get the money for a plane fare, she finally swallowed her pride and started hooking. Three months later, she boarded a plane for New York City. That was five years ago.

Julia dabbed at her eyes as she finished the story. "I started walking the streets near the Port Authority when I got to New York. The money was okay, but the guys were assholes. Everyone had an attitude and half didn't pay up. A black guy called Whammy appointed himself my pimp and got me into coke. I left midtown to get away from him and found a downtown service called Wall Street Escorts. They got me into sex working with a better group of guys. That's how I met Monica and Alexandra and made some friends. Richard Gere became my best customer and now he pays my rent. All I have to do is be there for him on the two nights a week he stays in the city. The rest of my time is free, and I make money from other clients to pay the rest of my bills. I sleep with who I want, when I want. I ain't Clair Huxtable but I can buy what I want and I'm in control of my life. I got it pretty good, at least for as long as my looks hold out."

I reached out and put my hand on hers. "Thanks for telling me this. I know it was hard for you."

"That's more than any man knows." Julia shoveled the last potato latke on her plate. "Professor, you're now more than a john. I've given you a piece of me."

I swallowed hard. Across the table from me was a wild and wildly flawed woman with a past that made mine look easy. In the two months since we'd first met, she'd played wicked games with me, stolen my money, and sent me to the hospital. If her aim were a few inches better with the wine bottle, she would have sent me to the hospital a second time. If she stayed in my life, something terrible would happen.

But she was also beautiful, funny, and smart. And now, on top of all of this, she had opened up to me and given me "a piece of her"—assuming that wasn't just a line. Maybe she was bad for me, maybe she was mentally ill. But maybe with patience and love she could overcome her past and get better. Maybe, just maybe, I could help her get better.

We bought two bottles of cheap wine and headed back to my apartment. Julia and Harpo cooed "birds can't talk" to each other a dozen times, as I poured wine and took off our coats. Over wine we talked about my "Saving the Hooker" thesis. Julia laughed about whether she could be saved by anyone, much less "a nerd with womanly soft hands" like me. We laughed about her johns, particularly Richard Gere, the old man who lamely attempted to vanquish me with an umbrella. He was a Wall Street manager with a family and a big house on Long Island. He'd been paying her $300 a week for nearly three years in addition to paying the rent for the apartment north of Chinatown.

"He's a sweet guy with lots of money. A lot of working girls don't ever find a rich guy like my Richard Gere. He just likes a little playacting before sex. Thanks to Richard, I know *Pretty Woman* better than even you, Professor."

She jumped up and kissed me hard. We made out for a few minutes, my hands running up and down her perfect body. Then she pulled back and took out a Tic-Tac container. She tapped two little pills into my hand.

"This will make you feel great, Professor. Take them now, honey."

"What are they?"

"Happy pills. I took two in your bathroom a few minutes ago." I hesitated. She leaned in, "Don't be a pussy. A hooker with a drug habit would never steer you wrong. Trust me, Matthew." She used my real name.

I didn't trust her, but I did swallow the pills. A deep sleep overpowered me almost instantly.

⁌——⁍

IT WAS midday when I woke up. I was naked on my bed. My head hurt. I had to pee badly.

I ran for the bathroom, aware of something pulling at my chest hairs as I hustled to my little toilet. The apartment looked funny, but it didn't calibrate right away. As I peed, I caught a sideways look at something on my chest in the bathroom mirror. But I couldn't see anything other than a couple of reddish lines.

I finished peeing. Shaking out the last drops, I noticed a taped-over cotton ball taped on top of my pinkie. I faced myself in the mirror.

The crazy bitch had written on my chest in red-brown liquid, "Don't fuck with me." It took me a second, but then I realized that she'd written her threat on my chest with my own blood.

I walked back into my studio. My television and laptop were gone; my phone was gone; my iPod and docking station were gone; my wallet, credit cards, and keys were gone; the jar that held my research funds was gone. She took my leather jacket and even the old bike that I kept in the hallway. I looked in the kitchen. Even my microwave was gone. The couch cushions were slashed, and the down comforter on my bed was slashed, too.

In the middle of the bed, next to where I had lain, was the box that held my *Pretty Woman* DVD. The DVD was broken in half and the image of Julia Roberts torn out from the cover. I held the broken DVD and wondered what more could she do? Then a terrible shiver came over me. I jumped over my bed to check on Harpo. He was lying on his side on the bottom of his cage. I don't know what that bitch did to him, but he was stiff as a board.

My head hurt and a deep pain came bubbling up through my throat. Like a gibbering baboon, I whimpered and wailed until I fell into a fitful sleep.

Conversation with Dad: November 18, 2012

Lacking a phone, I lost touch with Dad for a couple of weeks. I finally called him from the center, in the little basement office that Randy and I shared (a place neither of us ever used). Judging from its five-by-twelve-foot dimensions and wall-length shelves on one side, I imagine that our office was built to be a pantry.

"Hello, who's this?" Dad sounded suspicious.

"It's Matthew, your son, Dad."

"Matty? Hey, what are you doin' calling from a 212 area code? You always call me on your cell, from the good ole 815 area code. It's one of the last bits of evidence that my son was born and raised in the heartland of America."

"Yeah, I know, Dad. I think John Mellencamp is writing a rock-opera about the 815 area code." I exhaled. "I lost my cell phone and haven't replaced it yet."

"Oh, well you better do that. Get a smartphone so you can read my petition-of-the-week the moment I post it. I haven't seen your signature on the last two."

"Sorry, Dad, I've been off the Internet for a while. What's your latest cause?"

"So, I got one up there now about keeping the government out of the tattoo business. Jeff Weller wrote it and I posted it. Stops those busybodies in Springfield from raising the state's age for tats to 21."

"Well, Dad, I don't think your crusade to preserve tats for nineteen-year-olds will make me spend $400 on a smartphone. I'll just buy another low-end cell phone."

"And maybe a landline, too?"

"I don't think so, Dad. I don't need a landline."

"I can't understand why your generation doesn't believe in having a real telephone with a cord in your home. Can't lose that kind of phone."

"Yeah, I guess so, Dad. Don't worry, I'm on a landline now from my office at the center. This phone's so old it has a curlicue cord—like we used to have in the house on Aurora Avenue when I was growing up."

"Oh, Aurora Avenue? We had some good times in that house. Your mother was good during those years. Hey, that reminds me, did Julia come looking for you yet?"

"Yes, Dad. She did."

"Are you keepin' your distance?"

"I am now, Dad. But we had another tough incident."

"How tough?"

"Well, Dad, I'm embarrassed to say this, but she's the reason I don't have my phone. I don't have some other things either."

"Shit, Matty, she robbed you. You need to go to the police. File a report. She could be dangerous. Get a restraining order."

"She is dangerous, Dad. But she's done with me. It took some thinking, but I understand her now. She's won. For her, it was always about beating me—controlling the man or destroying him. It was about getting my money and leaving me on her terms. Now that she's done that, I won't be seeing her again."

"Maybe, but how do you know you're right? Go to the police and protect yourself."

"Dad, I can't go to the police without revealing some things that don't look good for me either. My hands aren't entirely clean."

"Jesus, Matty. Don't even tell me the details. Just come home. I'm sending you a plane ticket today."

"Dad, I can't come home. I just need a little money, $1,000, to cover what she's taken out of my research fund and get my life back under control. I will lose everything if I come home now."

Dad's voice amped up, "It sounds like you're in danger of losing everything if you stay there. And I'm talking about more than your money and your stupid hooker fellowship."

"Stupid fellowship? Oh that's nice." I slammed the receiver down into the cradle. The best thing about the old landline phones—and something that Dad forgot to mention—is that you can end a call with an emphatic slam.

CHAPTER 10

Where the Third World Meets the Nerd World

Fortunately, because all of my research had been previously e-mailed to Randy, Dr. Beckwith, or the IRB, the theft of my laptop was not a tragedy. Once I could get myself to a computer, I'd just need an hour to pull a bunch of files out of the sent folder of my e-mail account, and download them to a thumb drive. But getting to a computer posed a minor problem. With no computer (or anything else of value) left in my apartment, I had no choice but to start working out of my little office at the center or the graduate school library on the Forty-Second Street campus. But I had no ID or keys. I spent two days fighting with the university to prove that I was, indeed, Matthew Hristahalios— a postdoc victimized by a psycho-hooker.

But that problem was managed, and without any distractions in my apartment or money in my pocket, my scholarly productivity shot upward. I filled in all the holes and completed my annotated bibliography by week's end. I spent two afternoons with Rachel and one of her grad students getting myself fully acclimated to the New York City social services that might be of help to the prostitutes in my study. While on site at a Catholic Charities women's shelter, I arranged my first hooker "interventions" per the previous referrals from Rachel's students.

Then, I started "saving" battered crack whores. I spent an entire morning bringing these women from social service site to social service site: health clinics, drug-addiction counseling, and vocational training programs. The hardest thing about accessing social services is learning where to go. Modern social services sites are in nondescript, off-the-beaten-path buildings, places where rent will be low. Usually, the buildings aren't even labeled. The New York City social services building on Sixteenth Street is nearly impossible to find, hidden behind the giant scaffold and rubble near the entrance. Other social services sites are housed in churches and parochial schools that make them invisible to the people most desperate for their services. Yet, even with nondescript and difficult locations, each social services site I visited was overwhelmed. The Great Recession had welled the client base for social services while simultaneously sapping the tax revenues needed to support their functions.

The hours of standing on line provided me an opportunity to really get to know the modern urban crack whore. Four of my subjects were black, two Latina. On the surface, the contrasts between these women and Julia were striking. Julia—a beautiful, tall, white woman—came to New York by choice. Maybe she was lucky, she attached herself to a wealthy john who treated her well and paid for her apartment. The crack whores now lived in shelters. They were born into New York City's worst housing projects and had never lived anywhere else. Five of these women were unattractive; their manner and speech were unshakably "ghetto." They walked the projects offering forty-dollar blow jobs or screws for eighty dollars. They accepted payment for their services in drugs, since the money generally went to drugs anyway. When desperate, the price of their services dropped to as little as ten dollars or twenty dollars. Two of these women had spent time living inside condemned buildings and other abysmal settings; three had been raped, including one woman who was gangbanged by gang-bangers. Another one was tossed down a flight of stairs by an angry pimp after she'd spent money from a trick on diapers for her kid. Two had venereal diseases, one was HIV-positive—none ever recalled making a john wear a condom. Two had babies living with relatives; neither mother had seen her baby within the last six months.

The week spent with these recovering crack whores allowed me a better understanding of something I had only read about: the enormous difference in prostitution based on race and class. For an attractive white woman who dressed up and found a steady, white-collar john, the life of a prostitute could be materially okay, at least for as long as the hooker maintained her looks. But for the large majority of prostitutes, walled off from wealthy patrons by race or locale, prostitution was a filthy, wretched life comingled with drugs, gangs, violence, and all the other trappings of modern urban blight. It wasn't a life women chose, but something that they backslid into after running out of all other options.

I developed a real fondness for one of the crack whores, Akeisha. Her circumstances were awful: She spent her nights at a homeless shelter, and her days standing in line for methadone in a valiant struggle to free herself from heroin and crack addictions. But I was impressed by her optimism. She'd decided that she was going to get well and train as a nurse's assistant. When she was clean and earning a living, she was going to get her daughter back. I started bringing her nursing books from the "free" table at the graduate student reading room, and I snuck her into the grad library once to let her see what a real college library was like. After our last afternoon together, I gave her a letter encouraging her to keep fighting:

> Over this past week, you've become my hero.
> As you go forward, you will have to be stubborn.

People will keep telling you that you can't be a nurse and that you can't be a good mother. You will have to be nice to people who are mean to you. You will need to bang on doors again and again. People will open the door only long enough to knock you down. You must pick yourself up, dust yourself off, and bang on the door again. It's the only way to achieve your goals.

I will be your friend, always.

Matthew

AFTER SPENDING the day with the recovering crack whores, I'd return on the train to midtown, catching Rachel around four. We'd debrief until five when she'd head home and I'd head to the graduate student study at the library to type up my findings. Each night, I'd sign in and go to my assigned computer. The graduate school made us wear nametags in hopes that this little step might somehow stir introverted grad students to become fast friends. The names on the stickers said it all: Gamal, Gurdip, Admed, Sanjeev, Ram. I was reminded of Will's wisecrack after seeing a photo of my NYU master's class: "Grad school is where the third world meets the nerd world." It was still true: of the thirty regulars who came to the study each evening, two-thirds were foreign. The remaining third were a collection of native-born doorknobs so devoid of personality that they made me seem cool.

I'd get back to Brooklyn about nine thirty, walk the two hulking Great Danes for an hour, and be in bed by eleven. It was an austere life, but it felt good. I was productive and vice free. I rarely thought about Julia.

BECKWITH SURPRISED me that Friday morning with a visit to my basement office. It was unusual for a senior professor to come to the basement, an ill-lit, ill-ventilated floor inhabited only by subdoctoral teaching and research assistants. Although the door to my pantry-turned-office was open, Beckwith knocked anyway.

"Come in Dr. Beckwith."

He did. He seated himself at Randy's desk with a grave look on his face. "Is Randy in?"

"Nope, haven't seen him. Is something wrong?"

"Well, it's probably better that he's not here anyway. Matthew, I have some tough news for both of you, but especially for you." He looked down.

I waited.

"The graduate school has cut the center's budget by 35 percent due to the university's continued cash-flow problems. The faculty is making some very hard decisions. Among them: We will have to cut back from two to one postdoc fellowship next year."

"Ouch. Gosh, Dr. Beckwith, I was really looking forward to working with next year's fellows. I know that the second years have a responsibility to work with the newbies. I guess Randy and I will be doubling up with our mentoring next year."

"That's only part of it. In light of the cuts, the center faculty conducted a full review of all nontenured staff, including TAs, RAs, and fellows. They made a recommendation to the fellowship committee yesterday about you. You were very slow to get your research on track. You may be turning things around now: Your last weekly report is very encouraging and your draft bibliography is impressive. Between you and Randy, the committee thinks your project is the more interesting of the two, but your progress, to date, can only be characterized as disappointing. The committee has no choice but to place you on a termination track. Matthew, your fellowship will not be funded after January."

My heart stopped. If I said anything, I don't remember what it was.

"Between now and then, you can still do a great deal of research and you have my absolute commitment to work with you on getting something publishable out of your work before it is discontinued."

"Is there anything I can do about this—some kind of appeal?"

Beckwith looked down, "You can seek restoration of your good standing and reversal of the termination decision. But I'm not encouraging you to do this. I just don't know if you really love American studies—it doesn't seem to be your calling." He put his turducken-sized hand on my thigh. "Take a couple of days to think about how you might want to wind down your work. There will be an official cancellation letter for you next week."

I TOSSED and turned most of the night. Sure, I was still funded for another two months and change; sure I could still list a prestigious postdoc on my curriculum vitae. But the premature sunsetting of the fellowship was a very big deal. It meant that I needed to get my ass in gear and finish my research by December, so I could write it up in January. I would also need to start interviewing for faculty positions. The job market is dismal for young academics, particularly those with quirky academic interests—and then there's the bias against white men in this era when colleges are desperate to create faculty diversity. I hate sending around resumes; I hate job interviews even more.

But, in a strange way, I was happy to have something significant to worry about. It would help me get beyond my hooker obsession. I thought about Julia only once that night, and then only briefly.

I went to the graduate student study first thing in the morning to draft the proposal for descoping my research. By noon, I had composed the timeline: Phase II of the research (proctoring prostitutes through social services interventions) would be compressed to two months. Then I downwardly adjusted my budget. I was all business and would have finished the project by midafternoon, had I not been interrupted by a voice at my back.

―――

"Hristahalios. Hello there. Dr. Beckwith suggested I might find you slaving away with the master's students." It was Randy.

I reluctantly turned toward him. "Congratulations on getting to continue your work for the full two years."

"I am sorry, Matthew. I know we've had our bumps, but your recent work tells me you have great potential. And I'm sure you'll catch on next year at a college somewhere that will let you pursue your research interests." Even while attempting to console me, Randy couldn't help being a dick: According to him I only had the *potential* to be a fine researcher, according to him I could catch on at a *college*, not a university.

"You're all heart, Randy."

"Well, maybe not all heart, Matthew. In addition to the fellowship, I have been awarded a grant from the Van Mater Foundation, a family fund started by the parents of an abducted child. They're committing $50,000 to expand the scope of my study to include the parents of kidnapping victims. Great news, but I will need a research assistant to handle the additional interviews and compile the resulting data for aggregation. Before I send an announcement out

‹ 123 ›

through the grad student listserv, Dr. Beckwith asked me to ask you if you'd be interested."

"Awesome news for you. And an awesome offer for me. It gives me the chance to be your chimp; I could perform simple tricks for coins while you grind out the music from your organ box. That's lovely. I can step three rungs down on the ladder to be like a master's student again *and* work for you at the same time—two great treats. Thanks Randy. I'm sure you'd be as great a boss as you are a colleague, but I have to pass."

"That's fine, Matthew. I didn't expect you to be interested."

I waited for him to leave, but he just stood there.

"Matthew, there's another reason that I'm here. I want to ask you about the woman I met in Chinatown, Julia Robertson."

I tensed up but tried not to show it. "What about her?"

"Matthew, please don't think ill of me for being concerned, but I don't think everything's right with her. I have a brother, Chandler, who's had it tough for a few years. He's a very avuncular fellow, full of amazing spontaneity and humor. Your Julia seems much the same way."

"So your brother, Chandler, can be the life of the party, like Julia. Is that your point, Randy?"

"No Matthew, my point is that Chandler is a drug addict . . . cocaine and speed mostly, but really anything. And your Julia behaved just like Chandler does when he's on something. If I was a little wooden in the restaurant it is because I was, well, irked by her conduct—I've seen behavior like hers before. Matthew, does your girlfriend have a drug problem? I think she needs help."

My head was racing: Was it really so obvious that Julia was high that day in the restaurant? How come Randy noticed right away? How might Randy use this information to further embarrass me in front of Beckwith and the other faculty? Was he angling to make me lose funding even before the end of January?

"You know, Randy, for the last three months you've behaved like my self-appointed older brother. Perhaps I lack some of your polish and you've interpreted that to mean that I need your help. Whatever it is, you're not as intelligent or perceptive as you think you are. I will take care of my relationship with Julia. And, for the record, you understand her a whole lot less than you think."

"Matthew, I'm not your foe. I'm trying to be helpful."

"See you later, Randy." I turned back to my computer and pounded out nonsense noisily until I heard him leave.

Conversation with Dad: November 23, 2012

It was Friday evening, seven thirty, when the phone rang in my office. The old-style bell deafened me, as the sound pinged off cinder blocks in the narrow, spartan basement.

"Hello."

"Matt. Is this Matthew Hristahalios?"

"Yes, Dad."

"Good. I got transferred to a hundred places at your pain-in-the-ass university before I found your phone extension. I kept saying, 'Please connect me to Matthew Hristahalios. He's a postdoc studying hookers at the center.' And the university operators hung up on me, like five times. I love you, Sonny Boy. But don't put me through this again. What's your number?"

"Dad, it's in your phone's memory. One week ago, I called you and you called me a commie for calling you from the Manhattan area code, 212. Remember?"

"Remember that you're a commie? I don't need to remember that. Every time we speak I'm reminded." Dad laughed. "Yes, I remember when you called me. But I don't know how to go backward on the phone display. It was easier to call your university and get connected to your office. At least it should have been—the operator didn't know anything about your center. Eventually, I was sent to the graduate school, which sent me to some department, which sent me to some other place, which sent me to three other places, until I finally got to your office because every other phone number in the university had already been tried."

"Your story tugs at my heartstrings, Dad. But why'd you want to speak with me on a Friday night? I would have called you on Sunday."

"I just found a super-cheap after-Thanksgiving plane ticket for you. Come home; I'll have your Aunt Rita make a great turkey. Nobody will care that it's a week late. I can get you from Newark to O'Hare for eighty-nine dollars."

"Dad, we've talked about this. I can't."

"What's keeping you in New York? A project about hookers that's done nothing but mess with your head and empty your wallet? A girl who's robbed you?"

"It's worse than you think, Dad. They canceled my fellowship. They're cutting me off on January 31."

"Christ, Matty. I feel awful for you. Come home. You proved you can get a PhD. You proved you can survive in New York for seven years. Now prove that you have a good head on your shoulders. Come home to a place where people care about you."

"I can't, Dad. I have a life here."

"You have nothing. Not even your fellowship. Name one person in New York who really cares about you."

I was silent.

"You're my son and I love you. I hate that I'm making you sad. Just name one person in New York who really cares about you and I'll drop it."

"Julia Robertson. She may be crazy. She may be dangerous. But she just might really care about me."

CHAPTER 11

Champagne for My Real Friend and Real Pain for My Sham Friend

Even as my academic life was falling apart, my home life was slowly coming back together. My replacement credit cards arrived. Davydos changed the lock on my apartment door and made new keys for me. And I finally logged enough laps around the parks with the slobbering beasts to buy myself a replacement cell phone—which I eagerly plugged in before heading off to the center. But the apartment remained an eerily quiet place, lacking television or Harpo's friendly tweets. The quiet was a constant reminder of the night I was drugged and robbed by the woman I could have loved.

That Monday, my status as a fellow went from bad to really bad. Beckwith's promised fellowship cancellation letter was waiting for me in my little mailbox at the center. The letter blandly thanked me for my interest in advancing scholarship in American studies. Then it offered to continue my fellowship funding through January 31st contingent on my "full compliance" with a long list of officiously worded terms and conditions. A few of the lowlights from that list are below:

> ▶ "You shall submit by December 24th a full accounting of Manhattan University funds spent, to date, on your research. To the degree that actual expenditures differ from

the budget approved by the Center for Interdisciplinary Studies on September 2, 2012, in amounts greater than fifty dollars, you shall provide written explanation for the divergent expenditure(s)."

▶ "You shall e-mail reports in a manner and format approved by the fellowship committee to Dr. Anthony Beckwith every Friday for the duration of the fellowship, unless a written extension is granted by said Dr. Beckwith, or his designee."

▶ "You shall complete and deliver thirty (30) written summaries of all interviews applicable to your fellowship research, consistent with materials submitted and approved by said university's Internal Review Board by December 28, 2012."

If there was any doubt whether the cancellation of my fellowship was more attributable to my lacking performance as a fellow or the university's budget troubles, the letter made it plenty clear. It was a sobering reintroduction to the word "shall."

Lastly, below all the legalese, in Beckwith's hand at the bottom of the letter, was the greatest insult of all:

Matthew,

Going forward, Randy will be your informal peer advisor. You should consult with him before submitting work to me or other committee members. I will have Randy report to the fellowship committee on your progress and his reports will help inform the committee's final decision regarding your continued support as a center fellow.

I am sure you will welcome his assistance.

My knees wobbled, and I propped myself against a column in the center's concourse to ponder my sorry state. I was ready to throw in the towel. I'd call Dad and beg him to buy me a one-way ticket to Illinois.

I headed downstairs to my pantry-turned-office to place the call. Things couldn't get any worse . . . or could they?

THERE HE was—the devil incarnate, Randy Skiles—sitting in our shared office for the first time all semester.

Randy was studying something on the computer as I entered. He turned to face me: "Matthew, I have wonderful news. My Suzanne is pregnant. We had planned to put off marriage and children until I finished our, well, my—fellowship, but I am still tickled. I will be a father in just seven months."

"Oh boy," I said without any enthusiasm. "Great news for you, Randy."

"Why yes, it is. And this is right on the heels of my foundation funding. With that support, Suzanne can even take some time off work to be with our baby." He beamed. "Come here, Matthew, look at these frequency distributions."

I leaned toward the computer to see a series of bell curves on the screen, each one with a brightly colored line covering the years 1970 through 2010. "Matthew, I have found a wonderful database of names given to American children over the past forty years and have arrayed the data longitudinally for the dozen names that Suzanne and I are considering. We want to select a name just as it's beginning to ascend in popularity. That way, our child will grow up with a relatively unique name, but have all the advantages of having a popular name by the time he or she is older. Suzanne will be tickled."

"That's great, Randy: A data-driven approach to naming your kid. I'm sure your child will tell his therapist that your research made him very happy."

"Why do you assume my child will be a boy? She could just as easily be a girl."

"I know that. Randall and Suzanne will give birth to the lovely baby girl Skiles."

"Why Skiles? I am planning to take Suzanne's last name. It is our small way of combating the steady drumbeat of subtle misogynies that still permeate American culture."

"Well, I'm sure you, Suzanne and your daughter will do a lovely job combating the steady drumbeat of subtle misogynies."

Randy stopped and stared at me. He looked puzzled by my sarcasm and frowned. "Matthew, I know you received bad news today, but, really, I would think you could be happy for Suzanne and me."

"Well then, I guess you're not the first person at the center I've let down. No matter. I think I'm done here. I'm heading back to Illinois."

Randy looked shocked. "Matthew, really? I hope it's not because of the letter. I lobbied Dr. Beckwith not to cancel your fellowship, without a path for restoration of good standing. And then I lobbied him intensely for a role in helping you get your research back on schedule. Matthew, don't give up. I will help you. All is not lost."

Now it was my turn to stare at Randy. The arrogant twit whose condescension overlaid all of our interactions was now acting like my biggest (and only) supporter. I theorized his angle: If I could save my research and fellowship, he'd get credited for the turnaround; if I bombed out, he'd get credit for trying to save a subpar colleague. Either way, he'd look like a good guy.

"I don't know, Randy. I think my goose is cooked with the committee. I'm behind on my research and overdrawn on my budget. I'm just plain licked."

"Tell you what, Matthew. Let's go down to the Blarney Stone and see if we can find a pathway out of trouble for you. If we can, that's great. If we can't, well at least I will have bought you a few drinks and paid small tribute to a fine scholar who will, no doubt, accomplish great things elsewhere."

Free drinks. How could I say no?

◦──✦──◦

TEN MINUTES later, I was in an empty Manhattan bar with a bottle of Glenfiddich single malt and Randy Skiles—just the demon alcohol, the demon, and me.

"You know, Hristahalios, we haven't developed the kind of synergistic relationship that Dr. Beckwith wants. Why do you think that is?" He poured a drink for me and one for himself.

"I don't know, Randy. Maybe it's because you say 'synergistic relationship' without any sense of irony. Maybe it's because you're a pretentious show-off seeking to raise your brand by diminishing mine."

"Oh, that's wonderful frankness. Good job, Matthew." If Randy was even the least bit put off by my broadside, he wasn't showing it. "But it's not true. If I were out to diminish you or your research there are so many jabs I could have taken. I was always restrained."

"Like what? Jab away."

"Well, first of all, Matthew, the hooker searching for a male savior is not as ubiquitous in American stories as you suggest. Recent American literature has started to emancipate the hooker: think about Cassie Wright in Chuck Palahniuk's *Snuff* or Wanda in Charles Bukowski's *Barfly*. Those are just two prostitutes who don't want to be saved. And then there's Aileen in *Monster*—she turns the whole fantasy of riding off into the sunset with Prince Charming totally on its head."

"Fine, but a few exceptions prove the rule. There's always a contrarian artist or two writing against the dominant narrative."

"Perhaps, perhaps not. But that's not my biggest concern with your thesis. Would you like to know my biggest concern?" Randy leaned closer.

"Lay it on me."

"You establish that there's a persistent male fantasy in Anglo-American stories, for example, saving the beautiful fallen woman. You suggest that this oft-told story is probably not well grounded in fact. And your research on actual prostitutes will document the gap between the fantasy and the fact. Is that about right?"

"Sure. I'm measuring the dissonance between what is real and what we think is real because of the persistent stories."

"Well, so what, Matthew? Why would I expect a storytelling fantasy to be grounded in reality? Whether your thesis is proven or disproven, its significance is lost on me."

"Wow. That's harsh. Why didn't you level that criticism at the center?"

"Because, as I've tried to say all along, I'm not your enemy. I've never been your enemy." Randy looked hurt. "Look. Because of my successes and your struggles I can understand that I must look like some kind of carpetbagger to you. But also understand how you look to me: You appear to be a lazy and unreliable researcher whose ill-fated postdoc threatens to tarnish the value of mine when the program gets canceled next year because of a second underperforming fellow in three years."

Randy poured a glass of scotch and slid it to me. "A toast originally offered by John O'Keefe may work well for us." He lifted his glass.

> *A glass is good, and a lass is good, And a pipe to smoke in cold weather;*
> *The world is good, and the people are good, And we're all good fellows together.*

"Yeah, nothing pretentious about that, Randy," I said, clinking his glass. We drank.

I raised my glass, "And here's wishing champagne for my real friend and real pain for my sham friend."

We drank again. Randy laughed, "Real pain for my sham friend—that's funny." I tried to resist, but I laughed with him.

"If you thought my last toast was pretentious," he winked, "try this one. It's from Lord Byron:

> *Here's a sigh to those who love me,*
> *And a smile to those who hate;*
> *And whatever sky's above me,*
> *Here's a heart for every fate."*

We clinked glasses again and drank.

"And if you thought my last toast was terse, try this one: Bros before Hos."

"You know, at Yale, we played a game that you'd like because it pokes fun at academic pretensions. The first player calls out two unrelated topics, and then the other player has a minute to develop a humorous journal article title linking those two topics. Would you like to try?"

"I don't know, Randy. It's fine that we're having a human moment with each other, but let's not . . ."

"No, I insist," he interrupted. "Please indulge me this favor. Call out two proper nouns."

"I don't know . . . Richard Nixon and Christmas."

Randy grabbed the pad he'd brought from the center and a pen. I poured two more drinks, and looked at my watch. "You have forty-five seconds left."

I watched Randy scribble, pause, and rescribble as he attacked the conundrum of a Nixonian Christmas.

"Ten seconds left, Randy."

"Don't need them. Here's the article title: *Dasher, Dancer, Prancer and Nixon: Christmas Imagery, the Nixon*

White House, and Passage of the Endangered Species Act, December 1973."

"Oh, that's clever," I exclaimed. "But why the hell would you know when the Endangered Species Act was passed? Who are you, Rain Man?"

Randy shrugged and smiled. "Few things impress faculty more than knowing the approximate legislative history for their favorite causes—so I've memorized Wikipedia pages for a couple dozen of the more significant laws from the Great Society and 1970s. It really helps at faculty cocktail parties. Your turn, Hristahalios: I'll keep it pretty easy since this is your first time. How about folk music and football?"

I grabbed the pen and wrote "folk music" and "football." Not sure what else to do, I started writing names of folksingers and football players hoping something would click in. I scribbled twenty names, with no leads. It was hard.

"Ten seconds left, Matthew."

"Shh . . ." Then it came to me. I started scribbling.

"Time is expired, Matthew. You lose."

"Keep your shirt on. Just a second more." I finished. "Here." I passed him the piece of paper:

> *Like the Fridge Over Troubled Water: Oversized Football Players, Diminutive Folksingers and the Inverse Iconography of Paul Simon and William "The Refrigerator" Perry*

"Bully for you, Matthew. Bravura performance. I'll drink to that."

And so it went . . .

A journal article about conversational English and Latin American revolutionaries:

> *Contradictions: the Impact of El Salvadoran Refugees on Norte Americano Spanglish*

‹ 135 ›

A journal article about flatulence and mathematics:

> Greater than the Sum of Its Farts: A Quantitative Examination of Potty Humor in the American Vernacular

A journal article about Star Wars and materialism:

> R2D2 and Are Too Me Two: Star Wars and the Rise of Movie-Inspired Bric-a-Brac

A journal article about Arabs and disco music:

> Sheik Your Booty: The Impact of American Dance Music on Arabic Culture in the 1970s

I thought about telling Randy that I had stolen this title from an old Frank Zappa album, but then thought better of it. The priss probably doesn't even know who Frank Zappa is.

By the time Randy and I left Blarney Stone two hours later, the scotch bottle was empty. He must have been hammered, because only a shit-faced Randy Skiles would put his arm around me and call out "Bros before Hos" when the cocktail waitress approached. For that moment at least, we were best friends. Even more shocking, I had committed to trying to save my postdoc with Randy as my mentor.

That same evening pigs started flying and the Cubs won the World Series.

⊙══╪══⊙

DRUNK AND alone in my televisionless and my Harpoless apartment, I flipped open my new cell phone. It was now fully charged and ready to go. There was only one text waiting for me. It was two weeks old and from "Unknown Caller."

It read: "I went 2 far. Sorry."

"It's ok," I texted. A reply came right back.
"Did u go 2 cops?"
"No."
"R U lonely?"
"No. Randy is my new BFF."
"Big surprise! Can i c u?"
"No."
"Y? ☹"
"Cause u r nuts."

Conversation with Dad: December 2, 2012

I called Dad that Sunday morning.

"Hey Matty. Whoa. I see you're calling from the 815 area code again. Welcome back to America, Sonny Boy, there's still hope for you."

"Yes, Dad, I have a new cell phone. And I feel patriotism and Pat Boone coursing through my veins again now that I am speaking to you from the 815 area code. What's new in Morris?"

"The shop's doing fine—I got an order to do a rebuild on a '65 Ford diesel. That's a great job, if I can ever find the parts—I sent Will to Janesville for the carburetor, but that ain't even half of what I need to finish the job. Besides that, you know that Morris is pretty quiet." Dad's pitch changed, "Nothing much has changed besides the young, hot celebrities moving in, of course. Madonna just bought the Russell place; Brad Pitt is now running the Farm & Fleet out on Lincoln Highway."

"Cute, Dad. But you're dating yourself. Madonna and Brad Pitt are really old. Try Beyonce´ Knowles and Bradley Cooper next time. They'll make Morris hip. On second thought, even they can't make Morris hip."

"You know, it's been a long time since you've been in Morris. It may not be as bad as you remember it."

"No offense, Dad. But Morris is the land of the undead: Zombies sleepwalk through the most boring lives. People are unaware of the world around them; they don't read books; they never leave Grundy County; they don't even realize they're zombies."

"It ain't so bad, son. People do just fine, here. People are happy enough."

"Mom wasn't happy enough, was she?"

Dad went silent for a few seconds, "Your mother, well, that's very different. She had a rough life, God rest her soul."

"How'd she die, Dad?"

"She was in a terrible car accident. You know that."

"I know that, Dad. But I also know that she was out on the road at one in the morning on a weeknight. People in Morris don't even make it through Leno's monologue at ten thirty. Why was she on the road so late that night, Dad? How'd she die is the wrong question. Why'd she die? Maybe that's a better question."

I heard Dad exhale loudly. "I guess you had to ask me sometime. I just didn't expect it to come up on a phone call. I always imagined telling you when the time was right, maybe while canoeing the Rock River or sitting on top of Starved Rock, looking down at the barges."

He exhaled again. "Here goes. After you left for NYU, it got really ugly between your mother and me. We held it together for a long time because of you. But with you a thousand miles away, your mother lost any reason to police herself. Her drinking went from bad to worse. I'd come back from the shop at four thirty and she'd be toasted. I'd throw her in a hot shower, make dinner, and then do the shopping. She stopped going to church, stopped tending her garden, and stopped doing anything for the house. On the advice of Father Dimitri, I came home one evening and demanded that she sober up. I told her that I was taking her to the recovering drunks' support group in Sycamore. Your mother wigged out and started breaking things. I grabbed her, maybe too hard, Christ, I didn't mean it. She hit me a bunch of times. Then I sort of lost it and I hit her back. I slept in your room that night. She snuck out of the house, sped off, and never came back." I heard tightness in Dad's throat. "I still wonder if I killed your mother."

"You didn't kill Mom. Morris killed her. It's just too small for someone like Mom. Morris would kill me too, Dad. That's why I can't return."

"Then maybe I need to come to New York."

CHAPTER 12

Purple Jesus and Black Santa

The night at the Blarney Stone was the high-water mark for Randy and me getting along. Soon after, my newfound BFF turned into a major pain in the ass. First, he wanted me to meet him each evening at his apartment in Riverdale, in the Bronx—something that would have doubled my subway ride and made me switch trains in Harlem. Next, he started sending me lists of questions about my interviews and methodologies. Even my annotated bibliography, which he had previously reviewed and liked, was now under his scrutiny. Each day, when I logged onto e-mail, there'd be a new list of pain-in-the-ass questions. Every question answered on day one begot three more follow-up questions on day two. Most annoying, he kept pestering me about basic tenets of my thesis—specifically the pervasiveness of "the hooker with a heart of gold" in American narrative. Each day, he offered a prostitute who didn't fit neatly inside the archetype—Holly Golightly in *Breakfast at Tiffany's*, Constance Miller in *McCabe & Mrs. Miller*, and Iris in *Taxi Driver*. We started arguing through e-mail whether the growing list of exceptions undermined my thesis. It was as if I were an undergrad and he was the teaching assistant with a hard-on for giving me a hard time. Working with Randy threatened to become a larger time suck than digging myself out of a hole with the committee.

It was Sunday, December 23, and I ignored Dad's calls. With only one day before my narrative budget and five days before my compiled research had to be turned over, I didn't need Dad badgering me about coming home. Instead, I sat down at the computer and outlined the grim tasks ahead:

- ▶ Reconstruct and document every dollar legitimately spent since September for which there was a receipt. (This accounted for about 10 percent of the funds in question.)

- ▶ Make up expenses, with narrative justifications for every other dollar spent, including money blown on my misspent nights with Julia and money lost from the robbery.

- ▶ Develop thirty plausible case summaries based upon the interview protocol and IRB package.

And there was Randy, still peppering me with daily e-mails about stupid shit in my bibliography. The only thing worse than having Randy as an enemy was having him as an ally, if that's what he really was.

I decided to ignore him. I went to the graduate library and started banging away at a spreadsheet. I had no template, no plan, and no desire to seek Randy's counsel. It was slowgoing. By evening, I had only accounted for about a third of my research budget. I'd need to pull an all-nighter to get the budget done.

I hated doing it, but I turned on my cell phone and texted Julia: "Need to pull all-nighter. Do u have something that can help me?"

The reply came right back, "LMAO. Thought you were a good boy. U need meth. C Purple Jesus."

"Who?"

"Purple Jesus. Go to Buzz Kill. He wears a Vikings jersey. Tell him u no me."

"Thanks."

"Can I C U? ☺"
"No way."

⁂

I TOOK the train downtown and arrived at the Buzz Kill about nine forty-five. The dark night was negated by the neon light and bright colors of the Alphabet City inhabitants in their evening costumes: '60s hippie, '70s funk, '80s new wave, '90s grunge fashions splayed across the old Bohemians who had, by now, forgotten how to look remotely normal. Suburban wannabees in their Goth fashions mixed among the natives. No matter the night, the streets of Alphabet City were crowded and interesting after dark.

The Buzz Kill was nearly full: fifty patrons, with at least 200 piercings amongst them. Although New York City banned indoor smoking years ago, Buzz Kill patrons still smoke indoors—and not just tobacco—without feeling the slightest need for discretion. Two gay guys were passing a joint between them as I entered. Mark Sandman's thumping bass guitar boomed through speakers in the ceiling. It was so powerful that I felt each note of the bass throb in my chest.

The Buzz Kill isn't large, so it was easy to find a guy in a purple and white Minnesota Vikings jersey. He was at the rear of the bar, in a booth near the bathrooms. He was a heavyset, light-skinned black guy; sitting across from him was another black guy in a Santa Claus suit.

I came up. "Are you Purple Jesus?"

He turned to me, "Yes, my son." He spoke in a reverent tone and crossed himself. "And who, my son, are you?"

"I'm a friend of Julia Roberts. She calls me the Professor."

"Well, a friend of Julia is a friend of mine. Yeah, you look like a professor. Is that a Brooks Brothers' shirt? Dude, where're your penny loafers?"

The Black Santa, across from Purple Jesus, offered: "Be nice to him, A.P. He looks too straight to be a narc." He let out a big Caribbean-accented ho-ho-ho.

"Sit down, Professor." Purple Jesus motioned for me to sit across from him.

But the Black Santa didn't move. "Sit on Santa's lap, little boy. Let's find out if you've been naughty or nice." They laughed.

I didn't move.

Purple Jesus nodded to his friend. Black Santa grumbled under his breath, "Just having some fun with this stiff man." He slid his big butt farther on the booth bench so I could sit down.

"So, you know why I am called the Professor. Just look at me." I tried to sound cool, "But what's going on with calling yourself Purple Jesus, my friend?"

"It's all about A.P."

"Your religion is new to me. I don't follow."

"The great Adrian Peterson, my friend, the greatest running back of our times, laid low by injury for two seasons, and now the savior . . . The man will break Eric Dickerson's record, carry the awful Vikings into the playoffs, and save our wicked world all before the New Year 2013. He carries us on his back every Sunday. And for this, we must all give thanks." He raised a pitcher with a purple liquid in it. "And here's the drink—Purple Jesus—too."

He pushed a glass filled with the purple drink in front of me and Black Santa. "This is the blood of Purple Jesus, my unsaved friend. Drink his blood and be saved."

Black Santa guzzled down a glass of the purple stuff. I waited.

A harsh look came to Purple Jesus's face. The playful schtick was done: "Hey, dipshit. It's just grape juice, Ginger Ale, and vodka. Drink it."

I did.

He became the cheery prophet again, "Now, you're in the Church of the Great Adrian, my friend. How can I help you?"

"Julia said you might have some speed. I need to speed through a week. Maybe, you know, you have something that could help me stay up for the next three nights while I stay, you know, effective."

"Effective is the word of the week, my man," Black Santa laughed. "You visit with Purple Jesus and he makes you effective. Just ask my girl. Last night she cried out, 'Oh man, you are so effective.'" The men laughed together. I fake laughed, pretending I found them entertaining.

"Okay, Mr. Professor, here's what I can do for you. I have some meth, a special kind of meth my friends call 'Tweakers' Delight.' It will lock you in, man. The Wall Street men love it."

He took out a baggie, showed it to me, and then stuffed it back into his pocket. "This is enough, my friend, to keep you locked in for a week. My regulars pay $250 for this big bag. But I like to give rookies a discount—and you look like a rookie. And it's almost Christmas, my man, so $200 for you."

"I only have one hundred forty dollars. No shit, Purple Jesus, I don't have a penny more."

"Man, you're killing me. Don't they pay professors? It's a sad statement about higher education." He poured himself a drink of his namesake. "Tell you what, Mr. Professor. You give me your $140 and give Black Santa a big kiss on the mouth, and we'll call it even. Black Santa likes you, I notice these things."

Black Santa gave me a smile and embraced me. His mouth came toward mine . . . fake Santa beard pushing into my lips. I felt his tongue probing at my lips. It took every ounce of strength to do so, but I opened my mouth and let his tongue enter my mouth. He tasted like alcohol and cigarettes. I closed my eyes until it was over.

Black Santa finally pulled away. "The boy don't kiss back, A.P. I don't think he deserves anything special for sitting there like a statue while a man tries to have a nice moment with him. Bad deal for Black Santa."

"Give the professor a break, Black Santa. He will do better the next time an attractive man kisses him. Seeing the professor freeze up like that is well worth the money, my friend." He took out the baggie again and put it on the table.

I picked up the baggie. "I snort this right?"

"Snort is an ugly term. Men of learning call it insufflation. What did they teach you in professor school?"

"Apparently, not enough." I got up to leave. "So, I snort this like coke and stay up for a few nights. That's the deal, right?"

"That's the deal. Go with God, Mr. Professor."

I TOOK the subway back uptown and headed to the bathroom of the graduate library's study room. There, in the oversized handicapped toilet stall, I took out the baggie of magic powder. There wasn't a good place in the stall for cutting lines, so I had no choice but to set out the powder on the toilet seat. Cashless, I rolled an index card into a snorting straw. It worked well enough: Soon my nose was on fire with a crazy new powder tearing new holes in my sinuses.

The drug was already upon me before I sat down at the computer. Every cell in my body was on high alert. The fluorescent lights in the ceiling screamed at me; the large nose on the Indian woman at the nearby workstation stretched toward me and levitated inches from my face. The white noise of the computer crackled like a fiery furnace, pushing waves of heat onto my hands as they stretched to touch down on tingling, ice-cold keys.

I pulled up my budget file and started typing new rows onto the spreadsheet. I banged out real, exaggerated, and fictional expenditures. I imagined travel expenses incurred while taking prostitutes out of state to visit estranged family members; I imagined paying $400 for comprehensive medical examinations and Depo-Provera treatments; I imagined retaining the services of a local health food store to hold healthy cooking classes for an imagined cohort of eight prostitutes.

It was so plausible, so perfectly congruent with the activities I might have undertaken had my heart not been stolen and mind twisted by Julia Roberts. I typed through the night, locked in on the spreadsheet. In retrospect, some of what I typed now seems unrealistic, but other parts were wonderfully imaginative and believable. The meth made me a bold but wily liar.

Sometime during the night, the half-filled graduate student lounge became empty, save the turbaned grad student sleeping at the check-in desk. I cranked out more and more speed-freak spreadsheet rows to the rhythm of his chainsaw snores.

Then the sun rose and started lighting the room. I had enough rows of imagined expenses to spend my budget twice over. The budget was due in two hours, and I needed to piss something awful. Standing at the urinal, I felt tired for the first time. I headed over to the sink and slurped water out of my cupped hands.

I sat down at the computer again and reigned in the more ragged and ridiculous products of the night's meth-inspired imagining. My head hurt and I was hungry, but I was close to something very good. An hour later, it was ready.

I banged out a brief note to Beckwith, cc-ed the other committee members and Randy, and attached the file. I hit send. I then found a squishy chair in a quiet corner of the grad student lounge and slept for three hours.

⊙━━━⊙

AND SO it went for the rest of the week. By day, I was a pale and studious member of the nerd world pounding away on a university computer in the graduate student library. By night, I was a soaring artist riding on the backs of Purple Jesus and Black Santa.

Beckwith and the committee ceased to exist. Frenemy Randy Skiles ceased to exist. The only thing that existed was the computer keyboard and me. I reinvented the crack whores at the Brooklyn women's shelters. I wrote up their lives as I knew them, but filled in the gaps with whatever came into my head. I documented the results of real and imagined interventions to help these women. They were now magically enrolled in job-training programs; one had just been hired to work in the kitchen of a restaurant. But for all the good I had done them in my imagined world, I remained realistic about their long-term hopes for success. They were works in progress and their long-term trajectories were unknown. For my research to be perceived as credible, I needed to balance success with the reality of the inner city.

I pounded out richly imagined stories about the other prostitutes I had met over the last few months based on scintillas of real life. Julia's friends, Monica and Alexandra, were remembered from their brief interviews at the Buzz Kill and reengineered into rich stories of drug addictions, innocence lost, social services interventions, and conversions into "honest" jobs as a beautician and a waitress now taking computer graphics courses through the University of Phoenix. The prostitutes I met at Julia's poker game were reinvented as female Horatio Alger stories: Each one, through my interventions, now gallantly struggling to free herself from hooking and bridge into a respectable occupation.

Even Ms. Caliente, the hooker from the entrance of the Holland Tunnel who I never summoned the nerve to talk to, was now saved by me. She became Juana Roberio: an impressive young woman from Chiapas, Mexico, who fled an abusive father tied to a corrupt local government official. She snuck into the United States in the false bottom of a cargo truck, enduring eleven hours packed like a sardine in 105-degree heat and total darkness. She came to New York to work in a Chinatown sweatshop, but she was forced into hooking after a shift boss attempted to rape her. Fortunately, Ms. Caliente had met me, and through my assistance, was now living in a women's shelter, where she found friendship and God. She was now helping women just like her to recoup their lives.

Finally, I turned to Julia Roberts: I remembered every word of her past from that night in the Polish restaurant. I wrote it up in exquisite detail. When there were gaps in her narrative, or gaps in my memory of her narrative, my imagination filled in. I wrote about my struggles to keep our relationship professional. I wrote that because she was so beautiful, vulnerable, and needy, I did once briefly succumb to her charms. I wrote a side note to the committee that I was submitting myself to the university for reprimand because of this breach. I wrote about her irrational temper swings and the violence she put upon me, including the murder of my beloved parrot. Finally, I wrote about breaking off all contact with her because she was too wild and too dangerous. I concluded my narrative about Julia this way: "Alas, some prostitutes are too twisted by their difficult past to step toward a brighter future. Some hookers cannot be saved."

By Friday morning, I had drafted thirty narratives. In eighteen of these narratives, my work with the women had progressed to the intervention stage where it was possible to determine if the women were on a trajectory toward being "saved." The eighteen narratives were distinct and well documented; they covered seventy pages. Somewhere in the flurry of activity, Christmas came and went. I didn't even realize it. That Friday morning, I reviewed and edited the week's brilliant and not-so-brilliant lies. I added tables summarizing my research results: seventeen hookers had taken discrete steps toward being "saved" and twelve were in process. Only one, Julia, had proven completely irredeemable. I included a methodological discussion of the qualitative research techniques employed, added an appendix annotating the range of activities that I equated with "saving," and added footnotes that discussed sociological and psychological pathologies encountered in each of the prostitutes studied. Finally, I included a statement on the difference between getting these women to embrace an intervention that might lead to "saved," and actually being saved. Maybe I was a fraud scholar, but at least my fraud scholar persona had a twinge of humility. A few passages were still rough, but the body of work—drafted in just five days and five Purple-Jesus powered nights—was amazing.

I was strung out and tired, but I cranked myself up on white powder one last time—one last surge from Purple Jesus—and read through the entire document again, tightening the narratives, enhancing the specifics around my interventions, and darkening Julia's evil side just a little more. It was eight thirty Friday evening when I logged back onto e-mail. There were eight unopened notes from Randy and half a dozen spam e-mails from hot singles wanting to date me. There was also a Christmas greeting from Will and a plea for help from the uncrowned King of Nigeria, promising me a rich reward if I helped him regain his throne with a $200 contribution. Lastly, there was a sweet note from Rachel Rubenstein offering to help me if I wanted to stop by her office. I didn't reply to any of them. At nine forty-five on Friday night, I attached my fictitious research results and sent it to Beckwith, copying Rachel and Randy.

I took the subway back to Brooklyn Heights, and stopped at the pizza place next to the tube. The meth and the week of sleeping only two or three hours a day had taken its toll on me. The person looking at me in the mirror of the pizzeria bathroom had bloodshot eyes and yellow skin. I wiggled my newly loose front teeth with the index finger on my right hand, and ran the index finger of my left hand over an ugly patch of fresh acne. I smelled my body odor. I hadn't showered or changed my underwear all week.

I ate four slices of pizza—my first food in five days besides a few bags of Combos. I entered my apartment, for only the second time the entire week, at one thirty A.M. Saturday. Besides waking up to pee a few times and drinking a few glasses of water, I didn't do anything but sleep until Dad called on Sunday morning—thirty-two hours later.

Conversation with Dad: December 30, 2012

I was still in a deep sleep when the phone rang. "Merry Christmas, Matty Claus, I tried calling you a few times over Christmas, but only got your voicemail. Anything wrong?"

"No, Dad. I just had to focus on writing up my findings. I worked all through Christmas, just logged onto the Internet once to sign your petition to the Federal Aviation Administration. Granting Santa Claus access to United States air space—that's funny. But I'm fine now. How was your Christmas?" I stretched and yawned a little.

"Christmas was fine. I drove to Kankakee to be with your Uncle Costas. He had a small heart attack a few weeks ago, you know. So I wrote the Santa Claus petition with him to kind of lighten things a little. He's getting along okay now. I can't believe that your professors made you work through Christmas. What's wrong with those people at your center?"

"Godless heathens and atheists like your son, no doubt. Don't worry about it, Dad. Christmas is just another day to me . . . worse than most, because all the decent TV shows are preempted for the baby Jesus. God's got rotten taste in television."

"I hate when you talk like that, son. Some time spent with the Lord would be good for you."

"Dad, how many atheists does it take to change a light bulb?"

"This isn't a joke from one of your atheist websites, is it?"

"Okay, I'll tell you. The answer is two. One to actually change the bulb, and the other to videotape the event so Christians won't claim that God did it."

"That's not funny."

"Okay, Dad, try this one. Why was Jesus such a bad hockey player?"

"Not answering."

"Because he kept getting nailed into the boards."

"Stop it, Matt."

"Just one more, Dad. How come Jesus can walk on water?"

"Please, Matty, I don't know why you want to . . ."

"Because bullshit floats."

That one got to him. "That's not funny." Dad was angry.

"Lighten up, Dad. If a no-good son can't taunt his Dad's archaic religious dogma, then I don't know what the world's coming to."

"Here's what the world's coming to, Sonny Boy. Your old man's booked plane tickets for New York. I'll be seeing you in about a month."

"Stay home, Dad. I'm not a little kid anymore, you hate flying, and New York ain't Morris. Dad, you can't even go to Chicago without freaking out. New York's three Chicagos in half the space. All the men have irritable bowel syndrome and all the women are on the rag."

"Too late, the tickets are nonrefundable. I'm coming the first week in February. This time, the joke's on you."

CHAPTER 13

Membership has Its Privileges

The first of the accolades came from Rachel Rubenstein via e-mail:

> Matthew, I read your case summaries over New Year's and was blown away. I am so proud to have played a small role in your efforts to help these at-risk women. I meet with my graduate students for brown bag lunches on Wednesdays. I'd like you to come talk with them if you can. Also, I have a friend over at WNYC who produces the public affairs program, *A Matter of Conscience*. If Tony Beckwith concurs, and I think he will, I will recommend you to her to discuss your work on the program. You'll need to de-identify your data, but that's easier than it sounds. Just give your study subjects names like Jane Doe, etc. I will help you if you need me. I can see your thrilling work being featured on *A Matter of Conscience*.

A day later, I received a call from Randy. I let it ring to voicemail. After he disconnected, I played his message:

> Matthew. This is Randy. Happy New Year. Your findings are most impressive. I want to let you know that I have already contacted Dr. Beckwith to convey my continued support for you. I think

you've acquitted yourself and your work. I am recommending the continuation of your fellowship. I am happy that I was able to help you, Matthew. Take care, my friend.

I nearly choked.

Then compliments came in from two of my committee members: Drs. Peck and Banjari. They called my research "substantive" and "powerful" respectively. But still I waited to hear from Dr. Beckwith, my committee chair and, apparently, chief skeptic. It was now clear that it was his decision to put me into academic purgatory, and it was equally clear that only he could release me from that purgatory. Judging by his nonreaction, he wasn't won over.

That Wednesday, I went to see Rachel's MSW students. We met in one of the lounges on the ground floor of her academic building. The chairs and couches in the lounge were big, blocky affairs, constructed to be too bulky for a stoned student to attempt to steal. I settled myself among Rachel's MSWs—eight young women of every race and hybrids in between. A couple of the students wore the uniform of the uptight feminist grad student: short hair, sweater-vest over a T-shirt, and lots of stupid politically correct buttons—pro-vegan, pro-sustainable development, pro-breast cancer (or is it anti-breast cancer?).

Rachel hadn't shown up yet, so I introduced myself and asked, "So, did Dr. Rubenstein share with you the abstract of my work?"

A few nods.

"Great. So we have a little time together to discuss prostitution and what we can do to support these at-risk women?"

"And men?" asked one of the uptight sweater-vests.

"Um, of course, to the degree there are male prostitutes."

"Of course there are male prostitutes," commented sweater-vest number two.

"Yes, I know, I met two in my research. I mean that prostitution, for better or worse, is a mostly female line of work."

"Yes," commented sweater-vest number one, "because men have a sense of entitlement about having sex whenever they want." I felt a bead of sweat on my collar.

I tried to win them over. "I totally agree. And even more so, men have created a dominant story about these women. The fictional prostitute is Cinderella and she needs to be saved by Prince Charming."

A few affirmative nods.

But sweater-vest number two, she of the shortest hair and the most political buttons, was not mollified. "I don't mean to be rude, but isn't there something a little misogynistic about your research? I mean, here's a highly educated man meeting prostitutes and seeking to liberate them. What if they've determined that prostitution is empowering? That can be the case when no pimp's involved. What if prostitution's their ticket out of poverty? Maybe she thinks it beats working two minimum-wage jobs a day, every day. There's just something a little disquieting about a man sitting in judgment of these women. As social workers, we support and empower anyone who needs help, but we don't judge people. Your work does."

More sweat on my collar. But Rachel came to my rescue as she sat down behind sweater-vest number two, "Let's not grill the presenter. Especially a presenter who spends his days helping at-risk women. Manners people."

"Thanks Rachel, but I really appreciate this line of questioning. I grilled myself with the same questions as I thought about my project. And, as you know Rachel, it was only with your help that I was able to mitigate some of the challenges posed by this line of questioning, and get myself into the field with my research."

With Rachel in the room and in support, the sweater-vest insurgency was crushed. I would be gracious in victory and show the rebels that I was down with the struggle.

For the next fifteen minutes, I told the MSWs that male hegemony, masculine iconography, and American machismo have continued to perpetuate the quasi-servile state of millions of American women. Prostitution was a manifestation of this. Even those prostitutes who earned a good living did so by selling their bodies, inherently degrading themselves to male patrons who likely degraded their spouses, female coworkers, and daughters.

There were now some approving nods. I pivoted to my research, and discussed my thesis and research approach. Rachel offered a few affirming comments as I spoke. The students started taking notes.

As the clock hit one, Rachel cleared her throat. "Thanks, Matthew. I really appreciate you doing this for the MSWs. Let's let them get to class, and perhaps, if you haven't eaten yet, we can grab lunch together."

"Of course, Rachel."

We walked down two flights of stairs to the small faculty cafeteria in the basement of the graduate school's main building—a room with 1970s wood paneling nailed over the cinder block walls to make the room look like something other than a basement. As I attacked the plate of indifferently prepared pot roast and mashed potatoes, I told Rachel about Dr. Beckwith's radio silence. She listened to my story in between crunches on her carrot sticks and romaine lettuce.

At the conclusion of the lunch, without me asking, Rachel offered to intercede. She leaned toward me, "Frankly Matthew, I don't think Tony's ever liked you very much. When he first introduced you to me, he told me you were talented but lazy. He wondered if you would go the same way as Derrick Lefettra, the indolent fellow who was cashiered from the center two years ago. A few weeks ago, he told me that he believed that you had squandered your budget without conducting much bona fide research. I told him that I was not privy to your regular reports, but that I was under the impression your research was progressing well. I told him I had every confidence in you."

She resumed her upright posture, "Then, when I saw your findings, I realized that even I had underestimated your progress and the value of your research. With this body of work you gain membership into a very special club: academicians whose work is making a direct, positive impact on at-risk people. Membership has its privileges; it entitles you to my friendship and advocacy." She gave me a serious look, "Tony is brilliant, and he takes his role as guardian of the Center for Interdisciplinary Studies very seriously. I admire that. But he's a very stubborn man who is prone to follow his instincts more than the information right in front of his eyes. Let me talk to him."

Two days later an e-mail arrived from Dr. Beckwith.

Matthew,

> Drs. Peck, Banjari, and I have reviewed your preliminary findings, conferred with Randy, and received additional information from other university faculty familiar with your work. Although there remain differences of opinion within the committee, we have decided to reinstate your fellowship for the remainder of the academic year. The committee will conduct an additional review of your progress in May to determine that your progress merits a second year. Pending a satisfactory outcome, your good standing as a fellow at the Center for Interdisciplinary Studies will be fully restored.

Your stipend and research budget for the semester beginning January 22nd are restored effective immediately.

Tony

PS: On a personal note, I want you to reflect on what forced the committee to nearly turn you out of the program. When ready, please come to see me so we can discuss this.

PPS: Rachel asked me about a potential appearance she might seek for you on a public affairs television program. It's fine with me. Just fill out the forms with the IRB and the graduate school publicity office. Good luck.

Beckwith's note was copied to the committee members, Randy, Rachel, and the university attorney who had drafted the letter that nearly ruined my life.

⁂

THE NEXT week was amazing. Rachel contacted *A Matter of Conscience*, and, just two days later, I was asked to come in for a taping of the show.

With Rachel at my side, we walked to the Empire State Building. Eight years in New York City and this was my first trip to its most famous building. I was expecting a palace, but the old building's lobby is tired looking. The public television studio, on the third floor, is no higher than my apartment in Brooklyn and the hallway only slightly more impressive than Uncle Costas's dimly lit dormer of his Cape Cod in Kankakee.

Nonetheless, I was nothing short of giddy as I sat down in the television station's tiny reception area. I was promptly greeted by an attractive young Asian woman, who gushed, "I am honored to meet you, Mr. Hristahalios.

Your work reminds me why I love working at *A Matter of Conscience.*" She gave me a pile of forms on a clipboard and motioned me to a high stool. She brushed my cheeks with makeup as I signed my name a dozen times on forms without reading them.

Next, I was greeted by Rachel's friend, Michelle Block, a short, pretty Jewish woman. She told me that she was the producer of *A Matter of Conscience* and a childhood friend of Rachel's. She described how the next hour would unfold: I was in the second of three program slots. I'd follow an imam, a rabbi, and a priest who cochair the grassroots organization called "Faith over Fat," a transtheistic crusade to rid New York City of big cups at soda fountains. To get myself comfortable with the program, I could sit off camera on the corner of the set, and watch the taping of their interview.

Michelle handed me the list of questions that I would be asked. The interviewer was Akanke Igwebwekwe, a fixture on New York City public television for twenty years. Michelle commented, "Akanke is a wonderful interviewer and used to working with people with little on-camera experience. She'll take care good of you. Just focus on her and the questions, and act as if you're chatting casually in her living room. She'll handle the rest."

Twenty minutes later, I walked onto the set with a petite gray-haired black woman in an Afrocentric smock. She smiled and we shook hands.

An off-set assistant waved frantically for me to sit down in the empty chair as I heard Ms. Igwebwekwe begin introducing me. "Good morning, and welcome to the second half of this edition of *A Matter of Conscience.* Joining me now is Matthew Hristahalios of the Manhattan University. This young scholar is in the process of studying New York's prostitutes and has apparently helped quite a few of them in recent months." She purred in a smooth, Anglo-African accent. Then she turned to me. "And good morning to you, Mr. Hristahalios."

"Good morning Ms. Ig-web-wek-we." The uncomfortable syllables sputtered from my mouth.

She chuckled good-naturedly, "Not quite, but more than half my guests stumble on my name. It is Ig-way-bweek-way."

"I am sorry, Ms. Ig-way-week-we-key-way."

She smiled. "That's good enough. Please call me Akanke. That is a little easier. But let's talk about your amazing mission to help New York prostitutes."

Over the next fifteen minutes, miss whatever-her-name-was and I spoke earnestly about my *faux* research. I had gone over the findings so many times that all of these mostly imagined women were now perfectly real to me. My narratives about them were clear and coolly delivered.

I felt as if I really were sitting in Akanke's living room. I made Akanke laugh with my *faux* self-deprecation: "You know, Akanke, in addition to helping these eighteen women, I did the people of New York the great service of personally draining some of the oldest, worst coffee anywhere in the five boroughs. The people of New York can all rest a little easier knowing that all the little diners and luncheonettes in our city's poorest neighborhoods now have a freshly brewed pot due to me."

Charmed by my good humor, Akanke deviated from the script. "You are funny, Mr. Hristahalios. I might encourage you to consider comedy if it weren't likely to divert you from your critically important work." I blushed, "I am just a shy grad student trying to help people. I hope nobody thinks I'm a hero." I was shoveling it better than Randy.

"Well, the viewers will determine who is and who is not a hero, Mr. Hristahalios. That is not my or your job. But I will say that it has been a long time since we've had such a young guest who is so tangibly making a difference in the lives of vulnerable people."

She glanced at her notes. "We have only a few minutes left, and I want to save that time to discuss the 'one who got away.' You talk about one woman in particular who was very special to you, but whom you were unable to help. Is there anything in particular you'd want to say about her. This woman you've named Julie. How did she escape your persistence?"

"Oh, yes, Akanke, there was one whom I could not help. I really, really tried. It broke my heart. But she has terrible problems including proneness to violence and the worst kinds of deceit. She robbed me and bit my finger so hard that it took several stitches to close the wound." I pushed my finger forward toward the camera and showed her the scar. Akanke Igwebwekwe squinted to see it and nodded.

"I pray for her," said a somber-voiced Akanke Igwebwekwe.

"I pray for her, too, Akanke."

"That is a very sad way to end our segment, Mr. Hristahalios, but I urge you to remember the amazing things you have done to make a difference in the lives of seventeen other vulnerable women. Please keep up the wonderful work. And please come back and talk to us again when your research is complete. I am sure I speak for the viewers of *A Matter of Conscience* when I say that we want to hear more about your work." She reached over and we shook hands.

When the red light flashed over the camera, I shook hands with Akanke again. She told me I was a great guest. Leaving the set, I was greeted by Rachel, who gave me a big hug. Michelle Block shook hands warmly with me and then hugged her old friend, "Thanks, Rach, for tipping me off to your protégé. He's a natural."

While putting on my coat, the hot young Asian woman who greeted me came up again. "Professor Hristahalios, I'm inspired by your work. I'm, um, Jodi Ng. If you'd ever want to meet for dinner or something, here's my card. I put my cell phone number on it, too."

Speechless, I took the card. Hot girls have never looked twice at me, but now that I was that perfect mix of Upton Sinclair, Edward R. Murrow and Mother Teresa, it would change—at least within the tiny demographic that watches *A Matter of Conscience*.

Jodi Ng and I became Facebook friends that night. We became real friends the next evening when I met her after work and began a two-part "Saving the Hooker Reality Tour." I gave Jodi a quick tour of the center, passing her in front of Jayaprada at the reception desk. I held hands with Jodi on the way in, and planted a little kiss on Jodi's lips in front of Jayaprada on the way out. The next evening, amidst a mix of snow and rain, I took Jodi to Alphabet City. She wore a long, puffy winter coat and goofy earmuffs that made her look like a little boy. Then I took her into the Buzz Kill and my eyes exploded as she delayered, revealing a skimpy red minidress and a perfect body. Seeing me stare at her sexy outfit, a grin came over her face, "Knowing I'd be walking Alphabet City, I figured I needed to put on something slutty." She giggled, "I call this dress Khmer Rouge because it could slaughter a million men."

We had a few drinks, and I sent a pitcher of Purple Jesus to the booth in back. Purple Jesus, still in the same stupid Vikings Jersey, stood up and we made eye contact. He called to me, "Power to the Purple Professor. Peace and Happy New Year."

"Hey, sorry about the last Sunday, my friend. But a glass raised to A.P. for a fine season," I called back to him.

After a couple of drinks, I walked Jodi back to her place, an uninspired building on the edge of the Village. We made out in the light snow in front of her apartment building. She told me to come upstairs with her. Though I wanted to go upstairs more than anything, I told her, "No,

I like you too much to go any further tonight. Please don't wear that red dress again. I won't be this noble a second time." We kissed again, and I walked away with a boner the size of a subway car.

That night, I was the cock tease to a hot woman who totally dug me. Imagine that.

※

THE NEXT day, Jodi forwarded me an e-mail sent to Feedback@AMatterofConscience.org. It was from a talent agent who wanted to speak with me. I texted the agent right away and we arranged to meet for dinner that evening.

I met Sandra Cardona of Schmitt, Simenauer, and Associates at seven at a SoHo bistro called Bazin's. The perverse charm of the Manhattan bistro, as best I can tell, is built around cramming dozens of people into a living room-sized space with stainless-steel walls and hardwood floors that amplify sound to create a deafening din. Hungry people then pay forty-five dollars for a tiny piece of fish wedged on top of a thin layer of caramelized arugula and underneath a bat-shit reduction. But at least the wine's good. I was halfway through a fifty dollar bottle of Pinot when my prospective agent finally showed up—35 minutes late.

Although we hadn't yet met, I could tell from her fast walk and clanking shoes that the intense looking woman coming toward me was Sandra Cardona. I rose as the hostess seated her.

Sandra Cardona looks like every other New York City businesswoman: black slacks, black blazer, black earrings. Her black hair is cut just above the shoulders and meticulously arranged to create the illusion of an unkempt appearance.

"It's a pleasure to meet you, Mr. Hrista-something-something. I'm going to call you Matt, if you don't mind. Sorry I'm late—the crosstown traffic is always bad this time of day, but never this bad. I will have to keep our dinner brief tonight—I have to get home and relieve my nanny by nine." She stopped for a second to inhale. "My assistant saw your segment on public television and was won over by your intelligent story telling. Then I saw it—and went WOW, this guy could be something." She glanced down at her vibrating smartphone. "You're not a New Yorker, are you? You have a Greek name, but you sound like Tom Brokaw, with those long, well-enunciated, mid-American vowels. Where're you from? Oh, where are my manners." She finally extended her hand to shake.

I extended my hand to shake hers, but she was already cracking open the menu and looking down into it. Not knowing what else to do, I answered her question. "Well, I'm from Morris, Illinois. A town of about 20,000 red-blooded Americans eighty miles southwest of Chicago, the seat of Grundy County, and home to one of America's largest corn boils—that's a county fair to the uninitiated. The town's motto is 'Nothing Ever Happens Here.' It's a good place to be *from*." Then I waited. Hoping my subtle dig at my hometown would be perceived as witty.

"We have a lucky strike, Matthew. It's still on the menu. I will order for us, okay?"

There was no evidence that she had heard a word I said. I nodded yes.

But she was already standing up and running off to flag down a waiter with our orders.

She returned to the table and sat down. "My assistant, Stephan, watches public television for me and records any guests he wants me to know about. He thought you were great, and, after watching the first three minutes of your segment, I do too. These stories you tell about helping prostitutes are awesome—philanthropy made sexy. That's perfect. And your Mediterranean looks and little sarcasms are perfect for the emerging Gen Y demographic. I have friends at Wolf News, the cable network. They're looking to highlight grassroots people making a difference—to remind America that the best way to help America's losers is through bottom-up efforts, not big government programs. I want to get you hooked up with Denny Spinks, a superstar writer who can turn your stories and notes into a book in less time than you'd imagine possible. Then we'll get your book published by Wolf News Press, and get you on Wolf News to promote it. *The Daily Howl* has a ton of time to fill each afternoon, and they love this kind of stuff. If you're any good, we'll sell 50,000 books in a month and get you moving toward a career in talk-news punditry. Sound good?"

If I said anything at that moment, I don't know what it was. No one in academia watches Wolf News. It's the butt of jokes. But I know it dwarfs CNN and other news programs in the cable television ratings. I had seen a couple Wolf News programs over the years, and was no fan. Every news story was bombastic; everyone sounded like Nancy Grace. And the talking heads at Wolf News certainly took shots at the same academic elite I was hoping to join. But I was as bothered by the liberal orthodoxy of academia as anyone at Wolf News.

The food came to the table: I had a tiny piece of salmon wedged between two pieces of eggplant (what is it with Manhattan and eggplant?) under a green avocado-wasabi sauce, with weeping baby arugula on the side. Sandra stood up, "You'll need to sign this. Please, I have to take a call." She put some papers on the table, titled "Full Services Agreement" and walked away. The ten pages of small-font legalese were impossible to read in the dark restaurant.

As Sandra kept talking to her phone, I calibrated what was being proposed. It was surreal, but the idea grew ever more interesting: Matthew Hristahalios would be a talk-news pundit. Why not? I'm as smart as any of these people, smarter than many. Maybe I wasn't a retired politician or journalist, but the PhD after my name gave me cred of a different kind. Not that it mattered much, but at least Dad finally would be proud of me—he watches Wolf News as his main source for information. I pictured him boasting at the VFW every time I demolished some opposing pundit. Yes, the idea was ridiculous, but incredibly appealing. I was hooked.

"Oh, Matthew. One last little thing. That line about Morris being a good place to be *from*. I like the double entendre, but it will bomb on television. You'll want to play up your small-town roots—your schtick should be that you're John Boy Walton and you've come to the big city to save hookers because your small-town preacher put God into you as a young man. And while you don't like to discuss your faith publicly, it's that faith that drives you to save these fallen women. To the Wolf News viewer, we need you to be pure. Also, when you talk about that one hooker you weren't able to save, you'll need to get yourself choked up. Tears and outrage, on cue, are requisite skills for repeat appearances on Wolf News. Please work on it. Okay?"

"Uh, sure, I guess. But I don't think I can cry on cue."

She looked at me earnestly. "Matthew, before we go any further with this, there is something you have to know about me. It's a little shocking and might leave you thinking less of me, but it is also one of the reasons that your stories resonate so personally within me. I have to level with you. Are you ready?"

I nodded.

A pained look came over her face. "Matthew, when I was ten, I was raped. The animal pulled off my pants and forced himself into me. It hurt so much, and it hurt even more after he was done. He said he would kill my mother if I told anyone. So I kept the horrible incident secret for ten years. When I started dating, it screwed me up. I let any man who bought me dinner do anything to me. I would just lie there like a dead fish getting fucked. I didn't care." A tear came from the corner of each eye, and rolled down her cheeks. She took the cloth napkin and turned away. "I'm sorry you have to see me this way. But I need you to understand that this forever changed me, and it gives me a very special connection to your work." She wiped away two more tears. "Some people say I'm cynical about life and my career. I don't think so, but if I am, I hope you now can understand why." More tears. She sobbed quietly into the napkin.

"Are you okay, Sandra? That's an awful story." I reached across the table, putting my hand on her shoulder.

"See. It's easier to cry on cue than you think, Matthew. You can do this, too. Just practice. Also, sign the agreement now, honey. I really need to go." She handed me a pen and opened the packet of papers to the final page.

I signed my name.

"Great. Stephan will be in touch with you soon to discuss our next steps. Please enjoy the rest of your dinner. Sorry I have to go. The nanny's waiting."

Conversation with Dad: January 20, 2013

Over the last two weekends Dad had called me four times. I let it ring to voicemail all four times. My life had been a swirl of bad news, now dramatically reversed by a swirl of good news. I didn't know how to tell Dad about any of it. I also hoped that a couple of weeks of silence might induce him to cancel his plans to come to New York.

And still the next Sunday morning, at nine thirty, the phone reliably rang again. Without looking at the caller ID I knew it was Dad. I let it ring twice and then, reluctantly, hit the green button to say hello.

"You sure have a fine way of making a loving father feel like he's just a dingleberry hanging off your ass, Sonny Boy."

"That's funny, Dad."

"I don't ask for much from you, just a little of bit of respect and a returned phone call every now and then. Why can't I get either from you?"

"Sorry, Dad."

"Yeah right. You know I don't like big cities, and I'm a nervous flyer as an old man. But I'm getting over both to come see you in two weeks and I need some questions answered."

"Like what, Dad?"

"Well, first, am I going to get us in trouble if I wear my Bears jacket in New York? I need to know if I have to buy a new coat."

"Why are you worried about wearing a Bears coat in New York?"

"They hate the Chicago Bears in New York."

"Don't worry, Dad. Chicagoans hate the New York teams because of the whole Second City inferiority complex. But New Yorkers couldn't care less about the Chicago teams. You're fine. People will see the big orange C on your black jacket and assume you're from Cleveland."

"Cleveland! What's wrong with those people? But I will believe you if that's what you tell me. What about bunk arrangements. You got room for your old man?"

"Of course. You'll sleep in my bed. I have a fine futon for myself."

"Am I putting you out?"

"Nah, it's fine. I sleep okay anywhere as long as I'm tired. What's the next burning question?"

"Will you be meeting me at the airport? I don't want to go down into the dungeons of those subways and I don't want some shifty New York cabbie who doesn't speak English driving me halfway to hell."

"That's just an old stereotype, Dad. New York cabbies are tightly regulated. The city hires secret investigators to pose as hapless out-of-towners to make sure that cabbies aren't running up the fares. It's true that most of them don't speak English as a first language, but it doesn't really matter because I will meet you at the airport. Just send me your itinerary. Any other questions?"

"Only one, Matt. Are you happy that your old man is coming? This is a big thing for me to do. I'd really like to know that you're happy I'm coming."

"It is a very nice gesture that you're coming, Dad."

"But are you happy I'm coming?"

"I worry that your travel will create a discontinuity on petitions.com. What will all the right-wing nuts do if you don't post a new petition each Sunday?"

"The thousands of fine Americans who sign my petitions will get over it. Besides, Danny Bublitz says he'll keep the petitions going while I'm away. And we're doing great on the Vietnam Vets Day petition—over two thousand signatures. Now, stop with the comedy. Are you happy I'm coming?"

"Yes, I guess so."

"Not too convincing, but I'll take it. How you doin' anyway? What's new in your life?"

"Same old, Dad. Besides writing reports for the center, nothing ever happens to me."

CHAPTER 14

Adequate is the New Excellent

As Sandra promised, I was contacted by Stephan Stalbach on Monday and we arranged to meet over lunch at a west side diner, a few blocks south of the center. Over Reuben sandwiches and killer onion rings we discussed the details of the "Full Services Agreement" that I had signed.

The good news was that the terms of the agreement were better than I was expecting. The document could have said that I was now legally bound to wrestle alligators while waving my private parts at the Queen of England. I got lucky.

Here's what it said, according to Stephan's patient explanation: Sandra or her designee (Stephan) now had full responsibility for all of my media bookings. They now had full discretion as my sole legal representative to negotiate any books, movie rights, or merchandise arrangements (merchandising arrangements, really?) related to my work products. But I had the right to veto any deal that sounded bad to me. I was entitled to an 8 percent commission on the first 10,000 units of anything sold, indexing to 12 percent for "blockbuster" sales of 1,000,000 units or more. Any required travel would be paid by them.

I gave Stephan a thumb drive with my hooker research files. He thanked me, and gave me a $5,000 advance that I wasn't even expecting. This celebrity pundit thing was going okay.

THAT EVENING, I was contacted, via e-mail, by Denny Spinks, the ghostwriter Sandra and Stephan told me would be writing my hooker notes into a book.

Mr. Hristahalios,

I am totally digging your accounts of saving New York hookers. If even half of this is true, you're an amazing guy. You've given me plenty of source material and I work fast. I plan to have a manuscript of your book for your review in about ten days. I will leave some blanks for you to fill in details, and add some details of my own that make for a better story. If any of my additions make you uncomfortable you can remove them. When I send you the manuscript, I'll tell you what I've done and set you to reviewing it. You'll tell me a little bit about yourself, so I can write some autobio material about you while you review the manuscript. I get a big bonus if we can get your book in print by February 15, so I am hoping you'll be super about turning around the material I give you.

I live in Hawaii and sleep late, so we can talk at night. You have my e-mail if you need me.

Cheers,

Denny Spinks

I read this e-mail ten times before deciding what to do with it. I was insulted, amused and titillated all at once. Twice, I wrote long e-mails back to Denny with a cc to Sandra Cardona, but they both came off as whiny when I reread them. I deleted both e-mails.

Finally, I forwarded Denny's e-mail to Sandra with a one-line cover note: "Your guy is pretty presumptuous, isn't he?"

The reply came right back: "Of course he's presumptuous. He's the best in the business. I know Denny. If he likes the manuscript, he'll wire himself up and work twenty hours a day until he's done. He's finished books in a week for me a couple of times. I'm going to book you on *The Daily Howl* on Wolf News."

I wasn't sure if that was a bad thing or a good thing.

THE NEXT week was wonderful. With money in my pocket, I paid off my back rent and finally replaced all the stuff Julia had robbed or destroyed. (All except Harpo, whose murder still hurt so much that I couldn't get myself back into a pet shop.) I took Jodi out on three real dates. We did wholesome boy-girl stuff: getting gelato and walking the High Line on the west side; going to the aquarium at Coney Island; catching a concert with a clever a cappella ensemble Jodi recommended called The Bobs. The show included a guy skat singing sitar to a song called "Slow, Down Krishna." It was a comic story of an Indian holy man who falls in love with a bimbo. The skat singing sitar morphs into Herb Alpert's low-brow classic, "Tequila." For the rest of the night Jodi and I skat sang sitar to American pop standards.

Jodi came back to my place and we slept together that night. It was beautiful, miles better than the lusty, drug-abetted sex with Julia. The next morning was just as nice. We strolled across the Brooklyn Bridge on a brilliant, unseasonably warm winter morning. After getting dim sum in Chinatown, I walked Jodi home.

Already in Manhattan, I took the train uptown, and stopped in on Rachel during her lunchtime office hour. We shot the breeze like colleagues. I was no longer the struggling grad student in need of her help. She now pronounced "Matthew" the same way she called Dr. Beckwith

"Tony." I now called her "Rachel" just as easily. The stink was off. I told Rachel about Jodi and thanked her for all she'd done to help me.

After three weeks of putting off his e-mails and voicemails, I finally called Randy. We chatted for a half hour about my recent successes. Randy conveyed only the nicest sentiments. Briefly, I wondered if I had misjudged him. Maybe he really was rooting for my success the entire time?

I sent warm notes to Drs. Peck and Banjari with links to my public television appearance. I lied by thanking them for their support during my tough times. They were indifferent to me when I was struggling and soon I would be indifferent to them—but not yet. Both responded with well wishes.

Even though my life was back in order and I was living off a bumper crop of good karma, I knew that I still had one relationship at the graduate school that I had to right. I screwed up my courage and went to see Dr. Beckwith.

⁕

COMING UP to the center's third floor, with its creaking stairs, I expected to make eye contact with Dr. Beckwith through the open door to his office. But his nose was buried in a journal as I approached.

I cleared my throat.

"Come in, Matthew," he said without raising his glance. "Permit me to . . ." he scribbled something in the page margin and placed a slip of paper inside the journal as he closed it. "There, I just needed to get through the historiography section of the new Jackson Lears article. Once you start, you have to finish. Matthew, where do you stand on the need for the historiographic introductions in journal articles?"

"Um, I don't know. I guess it's kind of expected at this point. So we write them because it's hard to get published without one."

"Yes, they are expected. But are they necessary?"

"To be honest, Dr. Beckwith, I don't really think so. Well, maybe sometimes, for essays that set out to synthesize previous research, but I doubt they're needed for the presentation of original research."

"But even with the presentation of original research, doesn't the scholar need to place his or her research within a context of previous research to allow the reader to see how he or she is advancing scholarship in the field?"

"Maybe, but not always, and not always with the name dropping of the same predictable icons, like, you know, Foucault and Geertz. I mean, it's so boring and predictable."

"They are two of the giants and the frequent citation of their work reflects that. Scholarship is about more than your entertainment. If you want pyrotechnics, go to the movies." Beckwith frowned and cleared his throat. "When we publish something new, we stand on the shoulders of people like Foucault, Geertz, and Leo Marx and Eugene Genovese, and the poststructuralists, and the cliometricians, and the rest. We hope to reach a new height in our field by standing on their shoulders and then hope that others will stand on our shoulders. I think that other scholars understand our work better when we create a lineage, a pedigree, of what we've studied as a way to provide context for our own research. Perhaps it's dogma, as you suggest, but I think it's also utilitarian. Matthew, what worries me about you is that you don't seem to have bought into our traditions."

And there it was. Three weeks after being restored to good standing as a center fellow, welcomed back into the fold by the other committee members, Tony Beckwith was still expressing his doubts about me. Only this time, his doubts were tossed directly into my face. He was calling me out. And now, finally, I didn't need to kiss his ass. My face flushed red with anger.

"To be perfectly, honest, *Tony,* I think a lot of what goes on at the center is pure bullshit. I think a lot of what's written in *The American Journal of American Studies* is pure bullshit. I think Randy's research into the racial underpinnings of media coverage of kidnappings is pure bullshit. I think parts of my own research are pure bullshit."

"I know that," Beckwith smiled as if unsurprised. "The problem is that you have a year and a half left on one of the field's most sought-after fellowships, a fellowship that I apparently respect a great deal more than you. What should a good custodian of that fellowship do with a young scholar who—despite his great gifts—treats his field of study as nothing more than a manner of subsistence?"

"I guess the good custodian could seek to reform the errant scholar."

"And when the custodian has tried that?"

"He could try some more."

"We both know that is an evasive and lazy answer to a perfectly legitimate line of inquiry." He leaned in. "What should the custodian of a prestigious fellowship do when he's staring at a fellow whose work he suspects is largely fraudulent?"

A shiver went through me; Beckwith was on to me. But I didn't really care anymore. "There's a big difference between suspects and knows. If this hypothetical custodian only suspects the hypothetical fellow, there's not much the custodian can or should do."

"Well, I think, the custodian is duty bound to express his concerns to the fellow. He should make sure the fellow knows that he has doubts about the fellow and the veracity of the fellow's research. He should tell the fellow that he might launch an investigation. Knowing this, what should the custodian of the fellowship ask of the fellow who's likely a fraud?"

"He should ask that fellow to resign voluntarily in exchange for the fellow retaining his good standing, rights to his research, and not getting brought into an unseemly investigation that might tarnish the fellowship."

"I think that would be an adequate outcome."

"Adequate is the new excellent, Tony. Do we have an agreement?" I extended my hand to shake on the deal.

Beckwith didn't move. "I will look forward to your letter of resignation within the next week."

I turned and started down the stairs.

"Oh, Matthew," he called. "I saw your television performance. Howard Peck forwarded me the link you sent him. You really have a wonderful persona for that medium. You told your prostitute stories with good humor and glibness—like the traveling salesman of old. Rachel tells me that you have great prospects emerging as a television personality." His voice lowered, "I wish you everything you deserve."

Never have I been so cruelly cursed.

Conversation with Dad: January 27, 2013

I was proofing the first draft of my book, the one Denny Spinks had just written, when the phone rang.

"Hi, Dad."

"How you doin', Matt?"

"Great, just another wonderful day in my wonderful life. How you doin'?"

"Well, I'm going to say something that I never thought I'd say to you. I'm excited to be going to New York City. Do you know why?"

"Why, Dad?"

"Because my son was on New York City television talking about hookers, and never told me. Who knows what else I'll find out when I go there. Maybe you're the mayor or quarterback for the Jets too."

"I could be the mayor. But I'm never going to quarterback the Jets. I throw the ball too straight for that job."

"Drop the sarcasm, boy. How come you didn't tell me? Jane Rezepka from the library had to tell me about it. She called me down and we watched you together on their computer. I was proud and entertained and angry and humiliated all at the same time."

"I don't know. I guess I should have told you. Sorry."

"That's not good enough. Why didn't you tell me? You don't tell me anything. It's like I'm always prying facts from you."

"It's just that it's always been a pain in the ass talking seriously with you. You never like anything I'm doing. You're always putting me down. At some point, children put up walls because they're tired of getting put down all the time."

"Geez, you're still a delicate daisy. But I'm sorry if that's how I look to you. You're my boy and I'm proud of you. You were great on that television show. The *Morris Beagle* is putting a picture of you on the front page with a little story about your television appearance. It's only public television—something I'd defund in a heartbeat if I was president and that's the subject of my most recent petition by the way—but it's still really good that you got onto that program. Maybe you'll be on *Nightline* or *60 Minutes* next."

"Or Wolf News, Dad?"

"Hell yeah, or Wolf News. What're you telling me, Matty?" Dad's voice amped up with anticipation.

"I'm telling you, Dad, that I will be bringing you with me to a taping of *The Daily Howl* while you're in New York. Pack a suit."

"Hot damn, Matty. That's my favorite show. You're a regular celebrity."

"I guess I am."

CHAPTER 15

It's Cheaper to Keep Her

I had a mixed reaction to the first draft of the manuscript, *Saving the Hooker*. My hands actually trembled as I held the 225 freshly printed pages. I was bowled over by the speed with which it was produced. Denny Spinks was nothing if not an industrious writer. I wondered if he was a speed freak, the way I was a speed freak for a week. He had taken my choppy sentences about my imagined interventions and prostitutes, and made them into a legitimate free-flowing narrative. Each of my prostitute files was now a complete story describing how I met the woman, what she was like, and whether she was responsive or resistant to being "saved." He wrote perfectly credible first-person introductions to each chapter. He inserted made-up details about my personal reaction to each prostitute, and dropped little made-up autobiographical snippets throughout each chapter. He skillfully slapped a veneer of fresh lies atop the original lies I gave him to create a credible whole.

A few parts of the manuscript were over the top and a few other parts were below the belt. Denny made me sound uncomfortably heroic: he told a story, for example, about me selling my own bone marrow at a sketchy clinic to finance the prescription drugs of one prostitute. I struck that out along with a few other passages that pushed me into Mother Teresa territory. I also cringed at Denny's naming Brooklyn crack whores "Brooklyn crack whores." At the time, Rachel's humanizing influence had prevented me from using such base terms. I've gotten over it since.

Most of all, I was uncomfortable with how Denny reengineered the chapter about Julia (called Julie in the manuscript). He made her into a sex addict, inventing facts about her falling for me. My notes on Julia had included admissions that Julia and I had "sexual digressions" and that my relationship "went beyond scholarly," but Denny overdid it. I made dozens of corrections to Denny's manuscript, including lessening my (imagined) resistance to her advances and including our brief moments of real friendship. I didn't deify myself, but I did add more detail to Julia's psycho flashes, drug problems, and dangerous behavior. On completion, it was more true than any chapter in the book, but a few pretty big lies still slipped through.

I turned around Denny's version of *Saving the Hooker* in only two days. My markup was e-mailed at eleven P.M. on Tuesday. When I woke up the next day, there was an e-mail from Denny waiting for me with a cc to Sandra Cardona.

> Dude,
>
> You work fast and I like your changes. I don't know why you tamped down the chapter about Julie, but that's your call. Attached you'll find the revised manuscript. It's been great working with you. Sandra is copied on this note. When you tell her you like the manuscript, I get paid and Sandra starts making you a star. It's been real. —Denny

I scanned the revised manuscript. It looked like Denny made the changes I requested. I wrote back to Denny and Sandra.

> Denny,
>
> This looks great. Thanks for the quick work. Re Julie, I tamped down that chapter because I want her on my side. She'd be a dangerous enemy. It's cheaper to keep her.
>
> Sandra, Pay the man.

I met Sandra and Stephan that afternoon at their office in midtown. They introduced me to the managing editor from Wolf News Press, an Iranian-looking guy who called himself Butch. I was also introduced to the man who would be my cover artist, a guy named Van with the spiky blond hair of a teenager, but the ruddy face of an old drunk. He had already seen Denny's first draft of the manuscript and was ready with two cover designs. One idea struck me as pretty conventional: Bold letters of "Saving the Hooker" but with the two O's in hooker turned into the male-arrow and female-cross signs—the arrow and cross intertwined. Hand-drawn prostitutes leaned up against a few of the big letters. Everyone said polite things to Van about the first cover concept; no one gushed.

The second cover generated real argument. An open laptop was superimposed over a blue-sky background. Emerging from the laptop was a pair of lovely female legs in fishnet stockings and high heels. Black metallic letters proclaimed: "Saving the Hooker." Sandra and Van called it "bold," "imaginative," and "attention grabbing." Stephan and Butch hated it, calling it "sexist," "creepy," and "fucked up."

Finally, I chimed in. "Those legs are hot and provocative, and sex sells." On that statement, everyone fell in line.

Sandra giggled a little. "See Butch, Mr. Hristahalios is all business. He can be the next Ann Coulter. Get the sexy cover ready and get distribution cranked up. I'll move up Matthew's booking on *The Daily Howl* to early next week."

My impending national television debut was only the second most nerve-wracking event on the horizon: The most nerve-wracking was Dad's visit, now just three days away. Thanks to Sandra's advance, the apartment was largely restored to its past glory, but that past glory was still pretty dismal. Of course, Dad wasn't expecting the Ritz, but I needed to do a hundred things to get ready for him, from buying nonsugary breakfast cereal to making space for him in the closet. And the apartment was, even when the junk was picked up, still filthy. I hired a maid, and then choked when I found out that I owed this tiny four-foot-ten-inch woman $150 for three hours of work. Only in New York City can an illegal immigrant earn fifty dollars an hour from a regular American who only dreams of making fifty dollars an hour.

But at least she did a good job. The apartment's wood floor was shiny for the first time in five years and the bathroom and kitchen tiles were white again. I had forgotten that the bathroom had white tiles when I moved in—recalling that they'd always been beige. A trip to the local hardware store resulted in shelves over the kitchen sink and a trip to the grocery store put food on those shelves. This created the illusion of a kitchen used for something other than microwaving leftover Chinese food. Fresh sheets on the bed, a new comforter, and, finally, a flat-screen television mounted above the mantle made the apartment appear downright homey.

Dad called twice on the morning of his flight. He called before he left the house to confirm that I'd meet him at the airport baggage claim, carousel number eleven in terminal A. Then he called from his cell phone at the airport to confirm that I'd meet him at the airport baggage claim, carousel number eleven in terminal A. When his plane landed, he called me again, from the runway, to confirm that I'd meet him at baggage claim, carousel number eleven in terminal A.

Twenty-five minutes later this old guy came down the escalator into baggage claim, head on a swivel, eyes darting nervously in all directions. In five years, his hair had finally thinned to the point where a comb-over was pointless—he'd crossed over from thinning to bald. Gravity had scored some victories on his body: his cheeks had slid down a little bit and his double chin flirted with triple-chin status. His posture was slightly hunched over. Still, for a guy a year away from Medicare, he looked good, even in the ridiculous black leather jacket with the oversized orange "C" logo.

I walked toward him. "Dad. Over here!"

His head swiveled again. He saw me and waved as he came off the escalator and dodged an unattended child.

"Matty. Great to see you. I told you I'd meet you at baggage claim carousel number eleven, not here. We could've missed each other. It's still three days before you become a television star and you're acting like some Hollywood prima donna. Next time listen to your old man."

"Jeez. Dad, don't you think that . . ."

"Caught you, Sonny Boy. The old man can still pull your leg whenever he wants. Come here you big dummy."

Dad and I did a brief man hug. I took his travel bag.

⁕

THE NEXT couple of days with Dad went better than I would have guessed possible. Dad hadn't been to New York City since he was a boy and—besides the predictable Archie Bunker schtick about being surrounded by foreigners—he was an eager tourist. To my amazement, I enjoyed playing tour guide. We spent the first day in midtown, walking around the public library and then the Empire State Building. After going to the observation deck, on top, I took Dad to the public television studio where my new career was born. Jodi gave us a tour and asked Dad and me to record a station promo. She then took lunch with us. Jodi, the child of Vietnamese refugees, loved Dad's stories about Vietnam almost as much as Dad loved telling them. I asked Jodi to join us for my appearance on *The Daily Howl* in two days, but she politely declined. When I asked her a second time, a sour look came over her face, "Look, that program is not my thing. I think that host is a creep." She looked at Dad, "I'm sorry Mr. Hristahalios. I know you like the program. I'm sure you'll enjoy yourself. Please excuse me."

From there, I gave Dad a dose of Vietnam nostalgia by walking him down to the USS *Intrepid* museum. Planes from the *Intrepid* saved Dad's squad during a firefight in Vietnam. He and the tour guide, another Vietnam vet, bonded like long-lost brothers. The one-hour tour took two hours amidst all the old buddying.

The next day, I walked Dad across the Brooklyn Bridge into Manhattan, which he reluctantly called "pretty friggin' impressive." We took lunch in Chinatown. Dad wouldn't admit it, but I could see that he liked the hustle of the place, even if he only ate from half the dim sum plates that landed on our table. Then we went down to the Battery and took the ferry to the Statue of Liberty and Ellis Island. At Ellis Island, Dad settled at a kiosk and took a carefully folded index card from his wallet. On it was a hand-written family tree. Slowly, one key at a time, he started pecking the names of our ancestors onto a computer screen, and photographed images of the Ellis Island records of our ancestors followed. On each name, he called "Bingo" or "hot damn," and then he scribbled information onto the other side of the card.

"I never knew you were into genealogy."

"Never had much interest. But when your Uncle Costas found out I was coming to New York he told me about these computers at Ellis Island. And this is the only chance for someone like me to really learn something about my grandparents. These are your great-grandparents, Sonny Boy, so you might want to take a look." I pretended to be disinterested, but looked over Dad's shoulder each time a new Greek name appeared on the screen, names that I hadn't heard since early childhood.

That evening, Dad read my book manuscript quietly on my bed while I prepped for my appearance on *The Daily Howl*. He stayed quiet and let me work. But, a little after midnight, when I turned the light off, he whispered. "Son, you did good by these women. I never really understood what you were doing at that center with these hookers. Now I do. I'm proud of you."

On Monday morning, the day of my television taping, I took Dad to Junior's, the famous Brooklyn diner. I ordered big breakfasts for both of us. Dad ate the fluffy pancakes with gusto while I picked at my feta cheese omelet. Dad, never a gabber, monologued through the meal to make up for my silence.

Leaving the restaurant, we piled into the Lincoln Town Car that Sandra had sent for us. Crossing into Manhattan, Dad quietly started singing, *"Movin' On Up,"* the song from *The Jeffersons* television show. I looked out the window and started whispering the song with him.

THE DAILY HOWL is housed in the Wolf News Building on Forty-Ninth Street and Madison Avenue. It is one of Manhattan's newer towers—all glass and stainless steel. The car pulled into a small driveway in front of the building where a muscle-bound black guy in a tight black sweater opened the door and ushered us into the building. Dad looked quizzically at me as this was occurring. I shrugged, "He's protecting us from the paparazzi, I think."

We were brought into an ultramodern lobby area, with a giant Wolf News logo and flat screens of Wolf News playing at all angles. A stunning blonde came forward to meet us. "Mr. Hristahalios, it is a pleasure to meet you. Let me bring you and your guest into our guest talent area."

"Guest talent area? Yeah, we got one of them at the Morris VFW," Dad giggled. "It's the spot where Danny Bublitz burps the *Star-Spangled Banner* before the Bears games."

Dad nudged me and I laughed a little with him.

The stunning blonde introduced me to another stunning blonde who introduced herself as the associate producer of *The Daily Howl*. She, in turn, introduced Dad to the VIP lounge, a well-appointed room with leather couches, flat-screen TVs on every wall, a bar, and an impressive seafood buffet. As an attendant came to him, Dad said, "Since I'm the father of 'The Most Interesting Man in the World,' I'll have a Dos Equis." He looked back at me. "Good luck, Sonny Boy. I'll be rooting for you."

The assistant producer brought me to a makeup artist, another handsome woman. She looked sternly at me. "This man hasn't even had a good shave, I don't get paid enough." But her severe look softened as I sat down in the chair in front of her. "It's okay, honey. I've seen worse."

Sandra Cardona came in as I was being made into George Clooney, or at least Rosemary Clooney. "Matthew, Matthew, is everyone taking good care of you? You look like a fine young media pundit: The fresh, new, intelligent voice of bottom-up philanthropy, the new spokesman for the Millennial Generation."

She put a finger on my right temple, "Aksana, honey, you need to do something about Mr. Hristahalios's simian hairline. Can't you shade this in a little?"

The makeup artist came at me with some black goop that was cold and slimy as it hit the edge of my hairline.

After finishing with the makeup artist, Sandra walked me down a hallway. "So, Matthew, here's what happens next. You'll go into the Green Room. About a half hour before your segment, the segment director will meet with you there. I've already given her the list of topics you'd like to discuss with Marie. And here, Matthew," she handed me a sheet of paper. "Here are a few points and a couple of cute phrases I'd like you to work in when Marie asks about your work." I took the paper. There wasn't much on it.

"Um, yes, I think I can memorize this."

"Of course you can. Just one more thing: When you talk about the attractive redhead, the one you fell for but could not reform, I need you to become emotional. Figure that each tear is worth ten thousand book sales. Only a fistfight sells more books on daytime television than tears. You can cry for me, right?"

"I don't think I can."

"Just promise me you'll try, baby. You're a pro. It's easier than you think." And then she was gone.

I SPENT about an hour alone in the Green Room, a little nine-foot-by-nine-foot cell, with nothing but posters of Wolf News personalities, a small refrigerator, and a flat screen televising the early segments of *The Daily Howl*. I texted Jodi, hoping she'd come to the taping. After a few notes went back and forth, she ended the discussion. "If I stepped on the set of *The Daily Howl*, there wouldn't be enough soap in Manhattan to make me clean again."

At the time, I knew of *The Daily Howl* as a lowbrow cultural phenomenon more than as a television show. It was a mix of loudly stated political commentary, softball interviews with second-tier celebrities and homemaking experts, and a sprinkling of freak-show exposés that ended in onstage brawls. The show was routinely derided by "responsible" media voices and hated by pretty much everyone in academia. But it was also a ratings monster and rumored to have pushed Oprah into retirement.

The Daily Howl ran for three hours a day, every weekday, from one to four eastern time. A one-hour program, *Howl Highlights*, rebroadcasts the show's best snippets at ten eastern. Marie, the host, was a grown-up child star, born as Marie Hartsdale. When puberty left her with a cute cherub face that was too small for her adult head, the acting roles dried up. At age nineteen she was washed up, and she nearly killed herself with cocaine. Then she got herself clean, became a personal fitness maniac, found Jesus Christ, and rekindled the public's interest in her by donning a bikini and catfighting another washed-up starlet on WWE *Monday Night Raw*. As the final step in her resurrection, she went to court to purge herself of a last name and landed a steady gig as the celebrity-gossip reporter on the start-up Wolf News Network.

Five years later, her program, *The Daily Howl* was cable television's highest-rated daytime show. She'd become famous for picking fights with liberal guests and then howling into the microphone as they tried to explain themselves. The crowd would reliably chant, "Mar-ie, Mar-ie" as she'd cut to a break.

In the hour that I watched, I saw Marie interview a conservative talk radio host who called Gabby Giffords "a whiner" and her husband, Mark Kelly, a "stooge of liberal interests" for their gun-control advocacy. Then I watched Marie do a cooking segment built around "the surprising versatility of white bread" and another segment on "the time-honored and endangered practice of spanking your brat." By the end of this third segment, I was pretty sure that I didn't like the experts who ended up on Marie's program, but at least Dad was in his element.

During commercial breaks, I went over Sandra's notes and scribbled a few of my own. I thought how I could make myself cry. I relived the saddest events in my life—the double frog humiliation of my high school date with

Vicki Werner, Mom's death. But I couldn't coax any tears. Sandra would be disappointed, but I was actually happy I wasn't able to manipulate my emotions on cue.

At long last, the segment director entered the room. Like all the other people who work at Wolf News, she was a stunning blonde—but perhaps ten years older than the others. She proctored me through a mock-interview segment and offered some very helpful little tips, including encouraging me to sigh and look thoughtfully at the camera to buy a few seconds. She told me to take Marie's hand and look at her eye to eye when I wanted to convey emotion to the audience. We practiced together, and she declared me "a quick study."

She walked me out of the Green Room into the studio, where I could see the control room, the two-hundred person studio audience, and the set on which Marie was holding court as two experts argued over whether or not global warming is a hoax. As the segment director turned me over to another person—yes, also a stunning blonde— she whispered one final bit of advice to me. "Marie loves it when her guests cry. Men get invited back if they cry."

An usher brought Dad out of the VIP lounge. "What a first-class operation," Dad offered as he came up to me. "Shrimp cocktails and top-shelf liquor. Marie, herself, came into the lounge to say hello to me and the other VIPs. Look, I got this autographed picture with my arm around her." He waved the picture in front of my face.

The usher patted Dad's shoulder. "Sir, time for me to seat you in the audience."

"Good luck, Matty," Dad said as he was led away.

THEN MARIE started howling, the audience chanted her name, and one of the experts was heckled into silence. The segment ended, the experts left, and Marie stood up.

I watched the segment producer give her a sheet of paper. She scanned it and stretched, "Jimmy, enough with the Punch and Judy routine on environmental stuff. Let Hannity do that. This is daytime TV. Bring me more fresh meat. I want more guests like this hooker guy up next."

She looked at me. "Come on out Mr. Hristo-blah blah blah. Holy shit. I have no idea how to pronounce this name, and I have to pee something awful."

An aide brought me out on stage. She handed Marie a card with my name spelled out phonetically as Marie hustled offstage.

CHAPTER 16

The War with the Whore

"Mar-ie! Mar-ie!" the audience shouted as Marie bounded onto the stage. She looked splendid in her bright yellow dress and signature red-framed eyeglasses.

I sat in a not very comfy chair watching the back of her head as she stood at the front of her set and talked directly to the audience, reminding them that "banning assault weapons will kill American jobs." She closed her "Marie Minute" monologue on gun control with a remarkably witty piece of ignorance:

> If guns kill people,
> Then pencils misspell words.

Then she howled into the microphone. The audience dutifully howled back at her as she seated herself next to me.

"Settle down, howlers. Your alpha female is ready to speak again. As our country slides toward ever-bigger government and European-style socialism, we become more complacent about our responsibility to help the least fortunate around us. We tell ourselves we don't need to help our nation's losers because it's the government's job. But my next guest, Matthew Hrist-O-hal-E-Os (she nailed it) comes to us with an amazing story. Mr., eh, Hrista . . ." The audience laughed a little. She looked at me, "Mista Hrista, that rhymes. Man you got a long name. Hey, I got

· 192 ·

rid of my last name. Can I get rid of yours? Can I just call you Matthew?"

I leaned forward and spoke, probably too loudly, "Um, yes."

"Matthew brings us amazing stories about personally intervening in the lives of New York City prostitutes and turning nearly twenty of these women—whores, drug addicts, and thieves—into people on their way to living honest lives."

Marie turned from the camera and looked at me (and into the camera immediately behind me). "Welcome to *The Daily Howl*, Matthew." We shook hands.

"So, what made you decide to help these women?"

"Well, Marie, living in New York City and taking subways late at night, you see all kinds of people, including a lot of women who aren't doing very well. They clearly need help. People like me, blessed with a small-town upbringing in a place where people know church and community, know we have a duty to help people who are less blessed. After completing my PhD last year, I was able to get some financial help from Manhattan University, and I devised a plan to help some of these women locked into terrible, destructive lives. Then I just kind of started introducing myself to prostitutes—a hard thing for a shy Midwestern boy—but I did gain their trust."

"Now, I imagine that most prostitutes can't be very trusting of men. Didn't they think you were just a different kind of creep? How'd you win their trust?"

"It wasn't always easy, Marie. One of the prostitutes thought I was a stalker at first. Others didn't know what to do with me. They offered me sexual favors, maybe because they thought I was too shy to ask, and that's what I really wanted. But in all but one case, I was able to win their trust. And once trust was established, I found these women were very happy to have my help."

"And what did help really mean for these women?"

"Well, it meant different things for different women. It started with getting them into clinics for medical care and addiction counseling, cleaning them up if they had venereal diseases, and getting them to practice safer sex. It also meant getting some into vocational training, and others into respectable paying jobs like waitressing, jobs which can pay pretty good in Manhattan."

"So, Matthew, now that it's been a few months since you've helped these women, how are they doing?"

"I have become friends with many of them. And I know they're doing better—out of hooking and making an honest living now. One is even starting college. [Sprinkling of applause from the audience.] And I am blessed and fulfilled knowing that I've made seventeen lives better and made some good friends along the way."

A murmur of "aw" sounds rumbled through the audience. Marie looked at the audience and said "Awwww . . ." to them. Then a louder rumble of "aw" sounds came from the audience. Then Marie went "AW" even louder. And the audience responded in kind. Then Marie started howling, and so did the audience.

Marie finally turned back to me. "Now would be a good time to promote your book, Matthew." [Laughter from the audience.] A large image of the book cover flashed on the wall behind us.

I sighed and looked into the camera, buying myself five seconds to shift gears. "Well, I did write a book about my experiences and the women I met. It's called *Saving the Hooker* and it tells the stories of each of these prostitutes and how I was able to help them. I wrote the book with the help of my friends at Wolf News Press. [Sprinkling of applause from the audience.] It will be in the stores in a few weeks but it is already available for order now. In fact, for anyone who orders in the next forty-eight hours from www.wolfnewspress.com, I will personally autograph their book."

"Yes, howlers, I've had a chance to see Matthew's book, and it is a wonderful collection of stories. Very uplifting, and proof that any one of us can make a difference in the lives of America's losers. Let's give Matthew a great big howl for his great work."

The audience started howling for me. Caught in the moment, I piped in. "And Marie, this has been such a great experience with you and your howlers, that I'd like to give you all a big howl right back." And then I let out a big, throaty howl that made the studio scaffolds shake.

Marie was shocked, but quickly gained her composure. "Well, we don't usually get howling guests. That's very nice, but I need to turn to one last topic. Matthew, while your work has been so uplifting, so meaningful to these women, you do need to tell us about the woman who was most deeply troubled. Tell us about Julie, the prostitute you couldn't help."

"Oh, yes, Marie. This is a very sad story for me. One of the prostitutes, Julie, was very special to me. We became good friends, we even briefly became boyfriend and girlfriend—to the degree a tortured soul like hers can ever have a boyfriend. I tried so hard to help her and really felt something special, something like love, for her. I introduced her to my dearest friends from Illinois. I even physically intervened to chase away her john. But, as I said, she is a tortured soul, haunted by past sexual abuse and drug addiction. All of my efforts were only repaid with abuse. She robbed me, threw a wine bottle at my head, and even bit me. See, look at my thumb."

A man with a small camera came on stage to get a close-up of the scar on my thumb.

I reached across and took Marie's hand, staring into the camera behind her. "I assume Julie's still hooking, still taking drugs, and still hurting people. For all of my efforts I could not save this particular hooker."

Marie made a tsk-ing sound. So did the audience.

"I only want to say this, Marie. As God is my witness, I'd give up anything to have one more chance with her— one more chance to bring her into the light." And on that phrase, two perfect little tears rolled out of the corners of my eyes and onto my cheeks. The camera zoomed in.

Marie stood up, leaned over, kissed my forehead, and whispered, "God bless you, Matthew." The audience was dead silent. I was still a novice television talk show guest, but I knew I had just hit a home run.

Marie walked to the front of the stage. A man came running out on stage with a stool. He placed it between Marie's chair and me.

"Howlers, Matthew's story has greatly touched my heart, and I bet it has touched your hearts, too. What do you say we grant Matthew his greatest wish? Let's give a giant Daily Howl welcome to the one hooker Matthew was not able to save. Let's bring out Julie. HOWL."

A round of spirited howls went up from the audience, replaced by a round of staccato "Mar-ie! Mar-ie!" chants. My body shut down: The lights started spinning, sounds became tinny and garbled, blood rushed out of my hands and feet and into my cheeks. Drops of urine dampened my pants.

Julia Roberts stormed onto the stage wearing a dark red dress that matched her hair and made her look crazy angry. She stared menacingly at me. I thought she was going to charge me. But Marie timed her return to the middle of the set perfectly to calmly greet Julia with a little whisper in her ear. Marie waved for Julia to sit in the seat she formerly occupied.

Marie settled on the stool between us.

"Well, I'm guessing this is kind of awkward for you, Matthew, but we've delivered what you wanted most: A final chance to counsel Julie."

My voice quivered. "Why, yes. What a terrific surprise. Hello, Julia. How are you?"

Julia just glared back at me.

"So, Julie," Marie came into the discussion. "Thanks for coming on the Howl today. Is there anything you'd like to say to Matthew?"

"I'd like to tell him he's a big fuckin' liar and a fraud."

"Whoa! Easy there, Julie. This is daytime television. I hope our censors got that one. Maybe you can simmer down and talk a little nicer. Pretend it's just us girls."

"Sorry, Marie. This Professor Matthew is many things, but he's no savior of New York's prostitutes. He set out to study prostitutes—like chimps or lab rats—but he's such a pathetic loser that he tried to date us. He got all twisted around the axle with me. Took me on what he might call dates, then we had sex and he didn't want to pay. Then he behaved like a jealous boyfriend. He never did a damn thing for my good, just for his own. The people of America shouldn't cheer for him or buy his lies. They should laugh at him, or even worse, just ignore him like I did."

I had to stop this. "No, no, she's the liar. She's the one who attacked me. She's the one who robbed me."

But Julia shouted over me. "You're just a pathetic loser, Professor. Tell Marie about your drug use. Tell her about the coke you sniffed with me. Tell her about when you texted me so I could hook you up with my drug dealer."

Gasps and giggles drifted in from the crowd.

"She's twisting things around. It's not like she says. She's only a hooker. Don't listen to her."

But Julia kept ranting, "Marie, this asshole even raped me when I was sick. This is your savior of vulnerable prostitutes."

Dad called out from the audience, "Marie, this isn't right. Stop this. This woman is Matthew's crazy ex-girlfriend. They broke up and now she's trying to run him down. Cut to a commercial."

"Are you kidding, old man? This scene will make me a superstar."

A camera swirled around and caught Dad heading down the aisle and coming toward the stage. A big stagehand met Dad in front of the stage and restrained him.

A deafening chorus of "Mar-ie! Mar-ie!" started up spontaneously.

Julia was hissing again. "Hey, Professor. Why didn't double frog make it into your book? Why don't you tell Marie and America when you lost your virginity? Tell them who you lost your virginity to."

Marie turned toward me, "Matthew, it seems like *Saving the Hooker* has turned into *War with the Whore*. Tell America. Is Julie telling the truth about you?"

I went blank.

"Matthew, tell America if you took drugs with Julie.

"Tell America if you purchased sex from Julie.

"Tell America if you lost your virginity to Julie."

I said nothing. The lights swirled around me, I was disoriented. I tumbled from my chair. I was on all fours on the floor in front of Marie. I put my head into her yellow dress to hide from the lights and camera.

"Fuckin' pathetic loser. Look at him, Marie."

I felt Julia's hands pulling at the back of my belt. "Fuck me, Professor. Rape me like you did in your apartment. Shoot me up with your Christ seed, Professor. Put the messiah into me." Julia was on my back pulling me out of Marie's dress, straddling me as she cursed me.

"Lost your voice, Professor? I guess that can happen to defenseless creatures. Remember when I lost my voice as you raped me? Remember when your cute little birdie lost its voice? Birds can't talk; birds can't talk. Ain't that right, Professor?"

I bolted upright. As I did, Julia tumbled off me and onto the floor at my feet. I grabbed her hair and pulled her head upward with my left hand as my right fist came hurtling downward into her face. I hit her two more times before I was tackled by a security guard and pulled off the stage by two others. The enraptured crowd shouted, "Mar-ie! Mar-ie!" until I was back in the Green Room.

Life after Death

Dad and I left the Wolf News Building without saying a word to each other. There was no town car waiting for us. We took the subway back to Brooklyn. Coming out of the tube, Dad said I needed to eat something, but I told him my stomach wouldn't allow it. So we walked silently in the cold back to the row house that houses my little apartment. Two police officers were waiting for me.

I was arrested for aggravated assault and taken into custody. Over the next two days, before I could get a bail hearing, other charges arrived. These included a litany of misdemeanor charges related to soliciting prostitutes and drug possession, and a felony rape charge. Wolf News went after me for destruction of private property. Sandra Cardona went after me for breach of contract—citing the moral turpitude clause in my agreement with her. Manhattan University came after me for sundry violations of university rules. Finally, Julia piled on with a "defamation of character" claim. The hooker who double frogged me on television while using every profanity in the book was offended that I had besmirched her good name.

I was released from a holding cell on $100,000 bail. Dad put up his shop as collateral to get me out, and hired an attorney to represent me. He returned to Illinois before I was released and then cut off all contact with me. He even dropped me from his www.petition.com alert list. Different media sources hounded him pretty badly for a couple of weeks. Dad made an uncomfortable appearance on the Howard Stern radio show after the show's producer cold-called his shop. But Will tells me that the exposure to Stern's five-million listener audience has been great for business. Dad still won't speak to me or respond to my e-mails, even six months later.

The televised debacle was replayed three straight nights on *Howl Highlights*. Other Wolf News programs played the clip no less than seventeen additional times, and also showed a clip of Dad's horrified face with the caption "shocked father of fraud scholar." I was the cause celeb for an entire 24-hour news cycle during which I was discussed on mainstream programs like *The View* and *Anderson Cooper 360*. My freak-out was posted on YouTube no less than thirty times and I'm told that I temporarily replaced the dog that barks "Ri Ruv Roo" as the nation's most commonly viewed video. Wiseasses across America now call the act of a man punching a woman a "Hristo"; the term is memorialized on www.urbandictionary.com.

Even serious news outlets took note of me. The *Wall Street Journal* editorial page used me as an excuse to blast academia; The *New York Times* editorial page used me as an excuse to blast Wolf News. Ever the opportunist, Randy Skiles reinvented himself as my benefactor and best friend as he opined about me on *A Matter of Conscience*. Then he wrote an essay-within-a-letter-to-the-editor about me that was published in the *Times*. With a little underwriting from his foundation friends, Randy parlayed his one-degree-of-separation relationship with me into minor celebrity and now hosts a weekly radio program on WNYC.

Julia Roberts used the welts on her face to earn a half dozen television appearances. I saw a few of them and have to admit that she's created a striking television persona that combines the sexy exhibitionism of a Kardashian with the self-destructive daring of *Jackass*. Her appearance on *Tosh.0* consisted of dissing me while putting small objects up her ass. The YouTube video of it went viral and made Julia a hero among the nation's primordial male undergrads. This was more than enough for the *E!* channel to build a reality show around her.

And if you're wondering, *Saving the Hooker*, propelled by all the publicity, enjoyed six weeks atop the the *New York Times* Best Sellers list. It's available on Nook and Kindle, and translated into five languages. Sandra sold the rights to the book to a major studio that is considering how to convert the *faux* vignettes into a cable television miniseries. The moral turpitude clause in my book contract leaves me ineligible for even a penny of royalties. Wolf News made a killing off me after nailing me for moral turpitude. Hard to find any irony there.

As for me, the attorney Dad hired was a competent dealmaker who did all he could to settle things out of court. I surrendered all rights to *Saving the Hooker* in order to get Sandra Cardona and Wolf News off my back. I agreed to make a $48,000 donation (the cost of another fellowship) to the Center for Interdisciplinary Studies in exchange for the university dropping its charges against me. I entered a no-contest plea with the city on sundry prostitution and drug-possession charges, which were converted into a time-served sentence by a judge who felt sorry for me. The district attorney dropped the rape charge because there was no evidence of forced entry, and the results from the rape kit that swabbed Julia revealed a cornucopia of semen samples. But even after that setback, there was no deal making with her. She wanted her day in court, which she correctly predicted would draw dozens of reporters, microphones, and cameras to her. I pleaded guilty to the assault charge and accepted six months in jail at Otisville. At the time of this writing, Julia's defamation claim against me is still pending.

It took me a few weeks to unravel how *The Daily Howl* producers got to Julia to set up the ambush. But now I know. Although she meant no harm at the time, Jodi spilled the beans. She shared the PDF manuscript of *Saving the Hooker* with Michelle Block at *A Matter of Conscience* in hopes of getting me a second appearance. Michelle had some concerns with the manuscript and forwarded it to Rachel Rubenstein. Rachel recognized that many of the "facts" about the renamed prostitutes were untrue; my greatest supporter smelled a rat. She let Julia know about the book and my coming appearance on *The Daily Howl*. Julia contacted the program and, one way or another, got herself booked for the ambush segment.

Like Anthony Weiner, my former congressman and erstwhile New York City mayoral hopeful, I was brought down by forwarded e-mail.

⚭

AFTER A period of introspection, I'm now dispassionate about what has transpired. The fact is that I was always more huckster than scholar—living off the diminishing returns of spasms of scholarly productivity. That's my fault: It's not too hard to be a successful academic if you do the work and kiss a few rings. I didn't do either consistently. My childhood left me with some scars, but I don't blame anything on my youth. All kids are fucked up in one way or another, and my Mom and Dad did the best they could with me and each other. The people I've wronged at the center are made whole, and Randy, Julia and Dad are all better off as a result of my misadventure.

This book you are reading, this second book titled *Saving the Hooker*, will save me more than it will save any hooker. It will pay off my debts and chase the first *Saving the Hooker* (which is only a collection of lies) out of the bookstores. Critics will praise my bare-all confession for unmasking the comingled frauds of my own career and of modern academia. And even if they don't praise me, they will talk about me, which is vastly more important than praise. My bawdy story, bluntly stated opinions, and coarse word choices are perfectly calibrated to capture the attention of the 19–45-year-old male demographic. Appalled females will vilify me in their women's studies classes and newsletters; they will roast me on their blogs. I will make an appearance or two on college campuses, and I will be picketed. This will make me interesting to AM talk radio, where right-wing hosts will praise me simply because feminists will hate me. A columnist or two will have an intern read these pages and understand the grand cynicism of my strategy. They will write scathing columns about me. I will egg it on. All of the noise will stoke the publicity furnace and enhance book sales.

Cable television producers will invite me on air to talk about my controversial past and present, but I will mostly talk about my new book and mock redemption. And if they don't contact me right away, then I will do something provocative in front of cameras, like maybe shouting at or picking a fight with some respectable women celebrities like cancer survivors Cokie and Robin Roberts. Then the cable shows will have to book me. If I do well in these appearances, I will catch on as a regular talking head somewhere. Cable TV loves its degenerate pundits—just look at Eliot Spitzer and Dick Morris.

Or maybe I will go back into academia. I have a great research topic: The death of the true-life love story. My thesis is that history's great love stories—Anthony and Cleopatra, Arthur and Guinevere, Napoleon and Josephine, even John and Abigail Adams—were never true. These narratives rested on incomplete information and the free reign of storytellers to make shit up. I suspect that John and Jackie Kennedy represent the last hoorah for the true-life love story: They were the perfect couple, at least until the facts were known. Cynical journalism and ubiquitous television ended our innocence—ended our ability to believe in true love. The Internet and the instantaneous cable news cycle assure that we'll never be so gullible again.

Proving all of this would make for one hell of a good postdoc.

Thanks

In at least two ways, *Saving the Hooker* was a challenging book to write. It was tough writing in the voice of Matthew Hristahalios, with all of his contradictions and half-baked contrition. It was tougher still packing a half-dozen sensitive topics—misogyny, academic dishonesty, political correctness, drugs, prostitution, sexual abuse—into a small book, and then treating those topics with a comic touch.

I was extremely fortunate that nine literate and intelligent peer reviewers helped me tighten and improve the manuscript. Sally "Lady Red Pencil" Ketchum and Judy Adelberg (my mother) provided extensive comments on word choice, sentence and paragraph construction, and flow. If this book reads well, it is largely attributable to them. Nicole Carey reminded me that sexism, even under a comic or scholarly veneer, is always objectionable. She pushed me to clue in readers to the intrinsic sexism in Matthew's thesis and conduct. Joe Donohue was downright surly at times, but very helpful; he helped broaden my depictions of prostitution and life in New York City. Chris Koepke, PhD, and Professor Jeff Adelberg (my brother) sharpened the passages on academia. Tom Miglino challenged me on character development and steered me toward more nuanced secondary characters. Rhonda Sturtz of the *New York Journal of Books* reminded me of the need to balance dark and light, and helped me find that balance. Mark and Deborah Zobel gave me a pat on the back at just the right moment—their kind words kept me motivated.

Marty and Judy Shepard, my publishers, continue to flatter me with their support. I am proud to be in their stable of authors. Finally, Joanne, my wife of twenty years, gave me the gifts of time and tolerance as I wrote this book. She shrugged and smiled as I web surfed for prostitutes in the middle of the night. Her trust and good humor were critical to *Saving the Hooker*.

MORE FROM
MICHAEL ADELBERG

"Michael Adelberg's honest, moving novel, *A Thinking Man's Bully*, draws easy parallels to television shows like *The Sopranos* and *In Treatment*. Echoing the back-and-forth banter between Tony Soprano and his therapist Jennifer Melfi, the novel consists of a series of fictive essays in which narrator Matt Duffy attempts to work through some of his 'issues' with his therapist/interlocutor. Duffy and Soprano are both from New Jersey, they're both fairly overbearing, and neither has much faith in the therapeutic process.

"The elements of his life that have led him into therapy were the suicide of a friend many years earlier and the suicide attempt of Duffy's son, raising a deceptively simple question: is there something about his personality that drives the people he loves to suicide? Or, more bluntly, is he responsible? As the novel progresses, he starts to recognize patterns not just in his own behavior, but in his son's. The apple, it turns out, doesn't fall far from the tree.

"Ultimately, it's Duffy's evolution that makes the story so compelling. Leavened with deadpan humor and wry observations it makes a highly engaging, bittersweet read. All told, a superb debut." —*Small Press Reviews*

Visit www.thepermanentpress.com

Available wherever books are sold, or call 631/725-1101

**Friends of the
Houston Public Library**

ADELB LOO
Adelberg, Michael,
Saving the hooker /

LOOSCAN
05/14